COLD STEEL
AGAINST HOT LEAD

The gunman had his arm around Bonnie Whitford's neck and his gun pressed to her temple. Skye Fargo, crouched behind a stack of crates, couldn't do anything about it.

"Throw your gun out or I'll put a bullet through her head," the man said. Fargo had no illusions about him. He'd do what he said.

"All right, you win," Fargo called out, and he threw his Colt in an arc to land on the other side of the crates.

That left the Trailsman without a gun—and with just one last chance.

Skye knew exactly how thin that chance was. It was as thin and as double-edged as the throwing knife that he drew out of the calf-hoster around his leg . . .

3.75

TWISTED
TRAILS

by

Jon Sharpe

A SIGNET BOOK

NEW AMERICAN LIBRARY

PUBLISHER'S NOTE

This book is a work of fiction. Names, characters, places, and incidents either are the product of the author's imagination or are used fictitiously, and any resemblance to actual persons, living or dead, events, or locales is entirely coincidental.

NAL BOOKS ARE AVAILABLE AT QUANTITY DISCOUNTS
WHEN USED TO PROMOTE PRODUCTS OR SERVICES.
FOR INFORMATION PLEASE WRITE TO PREMIUM MARKETING DIVISION,
NEW AMERICAN LIBRARY, 1633 BROADWAY,
NEW YORK, NEW YORK 10019.

The first chapter of this book previously appeared in *Blood Pass*, the eightieth volume in this series.

SIGNET TRADEMARK REG. U.S. PAT. OFF. AND FOREIGN COUNTRIES
REGISTERED TRADEMARK—MARCA REGISTRADA
HECHO EN CHICAGO, U.S.A.

SIGNET, SIGNET CLASSIC, MENTOR, ONYX, PLUME, MERIDIAN
and NAL BOOKS are published by NAL PENGUIN INC.,
1633 Broadway, New York, New York 10019

First Printing, September, 1988

1 2 3 4 5 6 7 8 9

PRINTED IN THE UNITED STATES OF AMERICA

The Trailsman

Beginnings . . . they bend the tree and they mark the man. Skye Fargo was born when he was eighteen. Terror was his midwife, vengeance his first cry. Killing spawned Skye Fargo, ruthless, cold-blooded murder. Out of the acrid smoke of gunpowder still hanging in the air, he rose, cried out a promise never forgotten.

The Trailsman they began to call him all across the West: searcher, scout, hunter, the man who could see where others only looked, his skills for hire but not his soul, the man who lived each day to the fullest, yet trailed each tomorrow. Skye Fargo, the Trailsman, the seeker who could take the wildness of a land and the wanting and make them his own.

*1861, the Montana land,
not yet a territory, where men
made the law, but where life
was measured by the length
of an Indian arrow . . .*

1

Something was wrong, the big man knew as he reined his horse to a halt. His lake-blue eyes narrowed as he peered through the night at the ranch house. A big house, he noted, long and wide, with a second floor over one half. And the building blazed with light from every window, the way a house looked when there was a big party going on inside. But there wasn't a sound in the night, no voices, no laughter, not the clink of glasses, no strains of music. Only a tomblike silence.

The big man muttered to himself and moved his magnificent black-and-white Ovaro forward with slow, cautious steps. He drew closer to the ranch house and saw that the front door hung open and the sign at the outer gate—SAM WHITFORD—CIRCLE Z—had told him he had the right place. He halted again and slid from the saddle, now just in front of the porch. The silence remained absolute. One hand resting on the butt of the big Colt in its holster,

Skye Fargo stepped into the doorway of the house and raised his voice. "Anybody home?" he called out, and felt slightly foolish in view of the bright lights all around him.

But only silence answered. He stepped into the house and found himself in a spacious foyer with a black-and-white tile floor. Beyond the foyer, the house opened into a large living room and he slowly took in large leather couches, a fine cherrywood table and solid chairs, sporting prints hanging from the walls along with fine drapes. It was the living room of a wealthy man, and amid the fine furnishings he saw a silver tray on a side table with three partly filled glasses atop it. The tray seemed ready to be cleared away.

Fargo moved further into the house. "Anybody here?" he called again, and again only silence answered. He stepped through a side doorway of the large room and found himself in a study where bookshelves and stuffed antelope heads lined the wall. A heavy desk occupied the center of the room, a lamp burning brightly atop it. Fargo started to turn away when he halted and brought his eyes back to the desk.

A man's foot protruded from under one corner. Fargo's long, powerful legs took him to the desk in three strides. He went around to the rear of the desk and stared down at the man who lay facedown on the floor, almost under a chair that had been pushed aside. Blood seeped through the back of the velvet jacket where two knife wounds had torn jagged holes in the garment. The man's thick, silver-white hair was spattered with red, and Fargo reached down and half-turned the figure on its side. His lips drew back tightly as he stared down at a face that had been brutally bludgeoned and now lay almost covered with blood. No swift blow to the head but a vicious beating, Fargo noted. The dead man was unquestionably Sam Whitford, his mane of white hair unmistakable.

Fargo rose and his lake-blue eyes narrowed as they swept the room. Nothing else was disturbed, at least nothing he could discern. He moved from the dead man, out of the study, and crossed a well-lighted, wide corridor to halt at a kitchen. Stacks of dishes were piled up on the sideboards, along with the remains of brown Betty and blueberry pie. There had to have been a party, he murmured, and there was one more way to prove it. He started to turn when he heard the sound—first a gasped groan. It came again and he strode to where it emanated from behind the kitchen table. Another figure lay on the floor, a woman's figure, a gray-haired, ample form that was clothed in a housemaid's uniform of black dress with a white apron across the front.

He knelt down and saw the red that leaked through her dress. Her eyes flickered open and she seemed to focus on him. Her lips moved, but only a small bubble of red came from them.

"Easy, now, ma'am," Fargo said. "Who did this?"

The woman's eyes seemed to focus on him, and she tried to form words but her torn lungs hadn't breath enough left. All she could manage was a last, gasped groan before her eyes flickered shut again, this time to remain closed.

"Damn," Fargo muttered, and pushed himself to his feet. He walked from the room, crossed the corridor, and strode from the house to the Ovaro.

He dropped to one knee and scanned the ground in the light that came from the windows. The wagon tracks were plain, at least six sets of wheel prints, perhaps eight, he noted, and rose to his feet. They completed the picture, at least part of it. There had indeed been a party, with guests who came and left by wagon. That likely meant womenfolk, couples invited for a social gathering. But when the party ended, someone had killed the host. Whoever did it had killed the housemaid, too, probably because she'd seen him. The killer had planned one murder and had to commit the second out of hasty necessity.

Fargo turned and started to go back into the house when the pounding of hoofbeats erupted in the night and the band of riders emerged out of the blackness, horses at a full gallop. He counted seven riders, a tall man with a hatchet jaw in the lead.

The leader fastened his eyes on Fargo as he skidded his horse to a halt. "There he is. Get him," he yelled and drew his six-gun.

Fargo flung himself sideways, crashed into the edge of the door, and rolled into the house as the fusillade of bullets smashed bits of wood from the doorjamb. He sprang to his feet just inside the house, his own Colt in hand, and saw another volley of shots slam into the doorway. He ran into a side corridor and down the narrow passageway.

"After him," he heard the hatchet-jawed man bark, and the figures raced through the doorway into the house.

Fargo swerved down a side hallway and careened around the next corner just as a man appeared from the other end. The man started to bring his gun up but Fargo smashed the barrel of the Colt into his face and he went down with an oath of pain. The Trailsman started down another adjoining corridor and saw two more figures appear at the far end. They knew the house, whoever they were, he saw, and he dropped to one knee as the two men raised their six-guns. He fired twice and both men flew backward to smash into the wall. They seemed to be holding hands as they slid to the floor.

At the sound of footsteps behind him, Fargo whirled and dived to one side all at the same time. The shot passed over his head by less than an inch, and he felt the rush of air from the bullet. His own shot hit the man full in the midsection and he pitched forward, both hands clasped to his abdomen. Fargo was running before the man hit the ground. He leapt over the groaning form, spied the staircase, and raced for it.

Fargo took the steps three at a time, reached the second-floor landing, paused to look down, and saw the hatchet-jawed man and two others at the bottom of the steps. He threw a quick shot downward, saw the men ducking back, and spun away from the top of the stairs to see that the second-floor corridor formed a dead end with two rooms at the far side. But he also spotted the gabled window in the middle of the hall. He ran for it while footsteps pounded up the stairway behind him. The small window led directly onto the roof and he yanked it open, pushed one long leg through its narrow opening, pulled the rest of himself after it, and paused for a moment. The rooftop had a slight slant to it and he started to scurry across the shingles to the edge, where he halted again. He saw the front of the house almost directly below him, the Ovaro to one side of the doorway, the other horses opposite.

"There he is," Fargo heard someone shout, and he glanced across the rooftop to the window where two heads peered out. "Shoot, dammit," the hatchet-jawed man barked, and Fargo threw himself flat on the rooftop as a shot whistled by. He let himself roll, grabbed the edge of the roof, and let his long frame hang down. He dangled for a moment and heard the others hurrying across the roof. He let his hands open and dropped, his body braced, and though he landed on the balls of his feet, he still felt the shock waves go through him. He let his knees bend, paused for another moment to let muscles spring back, and threw a glance upward. The man's head appeared at the edge of the roof, but Fargo had the Colt raised and waiting. He pressed the trigger and the man screamed as he toppled face-forward from the roof.

Fargo heard the dull, crunching thud as the body hit the ground, but he was already racing for the Ovaro. He leapt onto the horse, and the Ovaro, ever sensitive to touch and mood, went into a gallop immediately. Three more shots followed him into the night, all wild and far off target.

Fargo followed the road for a hundred yards and then swerved right to climb a low hill thick with red ash and buckeye. He kept riding until he came to a place where the hill leveled off, and he reined to a halt and slid from the saddle. He lowered himself against the light-brown bark of a thick red ash and allowed himself the luxury of a long, deep breath.

This had not been the kind of reception he'd expected or wanted. For two weeks he had been riding to meet with Sam Whitford, only to find the man brutally murdered along with his housemaid. Fargo let the gruesome scene hang in his mind again, mentally reviewing everything he had observed. He had wanted to return inside the house for a closer look when the night riders had arrived. The frown clung to his brow. The men hadn't just happened by. They'd asked no questions, given him no time to explain anything. They had come expecting and aiming to kill.

A cascade of questions raced through his head. He had to start at the beginning, at that first meeting with Sam Whitford that had eventually brought him here. He put his head back against the tree, closed his eyes, and let that time spring into his consciousness in its every detail.

He'd been in Independence Rock down in Wyoming Territory, where he'd just finished a job for John Anderson. It had been John who'd brought Sam Whitford to him, and Fargo remembered how he'd been at once impressed by the man's suave manners, the silver-white hair on a face that still retained youth, and a sharp-eyed steely quality. "John told me you were the very best," Sam Whitford had said. "And you're contracted to break trail for Ed Simmons, all the way down to New Mexico Territory."

"I am," Fargo had said.

"That'll take you into next month," the man remarked.

"It will." Fago nodded as curiosity poked at him.

"Then you'll be ready when I need you," Sam Whitford said, and took out a roll of bills. He peeled off a sizable number and pushed them at the big man across from him. "Five hundred dollars, to seal the deal and ensure you're taking the job for me," he said.

"That's a powerful lot of walking money," Fargo commented.

"It is, but there'll be a powerful lot of work for you to do," the man said, and ran a palm through the thick silver hair.

"What kind of work?" Fargo asked.

Sam Whitford smiled. "I never spell out my plans till I'm ready to move on them," he said.

"That's smart," Fargo said.

"But it looks as though I'm going to have to do some manhunting, and I'll need the very best trailsman in the West."

"Fair enough." Fargo pushed the bills into his pocket.

"My ranch, the last day of next month," Sam Whitford said. "In Montana, west of Crazy Peak. There's a town called Horsehead. Take the road north some three miles to a broken, crooked, bare-branched elm and turn left. You'll come to my place, the Circle Z."

"I'll be there," Fargo said, and that had been the heart of it. They'd talked some about mutual acquaintances and then Sam Whitford had gone his way, leaving the kind of money you didn't turn down without some damn good reason. And now, Fargo frowned, the man who had hired him, paid him that good money, had been brutally killed, and he'd been damn near shot. He wasn't about to turn away and hightail it, not after a posse of gunslingers had tried to cut him down without so much as a question. He felt a certain obligation to Sam Whitford, certainly to his kin, and he supposed there were some. A wealthy man such as Sam Whitford plainly was usually had kin. He'd stay, Fargo decided, until he got a few answers of his own. He owed that much to the man who hired him, dead or alive.

The Trailsman rose, took down his bedroll, undressed, and stretched out in it. There were things he'd noted about the murder itself, and maybe they were tied in to what Sam Whitford had said when hiring him. Maybe. But there was too little yet to do anything but waste time on fruitless wonderings, and Fargo decided that sleep was much the better course and he closed his eyes. Morning would be time enough to arrange his first steps.

He slept well, the night quiet, the red ash a thick leafy ceiling over his head. He woke when the morning sun filtered its way down through the foliage. He sat up and the events of the night were on him at once. He made plans as he washed and dressed, found a stand of sweet elder, and breakfasted on the berries. He'd seek out kin first, Fargo decided, and perhaps the best place for that would be the sheriff in Horsehead. He'd also tell the man what he'd found and how he'd been set on.

Fargo turned the Ovaro down the slope, reached the road below, and made a wide circle around the Whitford ranch. He paused to look down on it from a distant hill and saw only a few horses tethered near a corral. He rode on after a moment.

He had skirted the town during the night when he rode to reach the Circle Z Ranch, but he'd noted it was not unlike a thousand other towns, perhaps a little bigger than most. That assessment was reinforced as he rode into its wide main street and slowed the Ovaro to a walk. Horsehead had the usual collection of farm wagons, some big Owensboro mountain wagons with their oversize brakes, and one bare-poled timber wagon.

He rode past a general store, a barber shop, a blacksmith, and just past the center of town, a small bank. A dance hall with the name CARRIE'S BUNKHOUSE over the front door came into view, all places common enough in a town, but he was surprised to see a church with a thin steeple and a long grain-supply shed nearby. He wondered if the presence of the Sioux and Crow throughout the land accounted for even the church being centered in town. He was beginning to wonder about the sheriff's office when he came to it almost at the other end of town, a thin, frame building with a single window and a long hitching post outside.

Fargo rode to a halt, swung from the Ovaro to see the man emerge, a sheriff's badge on his checkered shirt, and behind him, a thinner figure sporting a deputy's badge. The sheriff was a medium-sized man with an oversized, bulbous nose, heavy-knuckled hands, and shrewd eyes that stared at him, flicked to the Ovaro, and back to him. Fargo glimpsed the thinner man move to one side, circle toward a horse tied to the hitching post. The sheriff continued to stare at him, Fargo saw, a frown digging into the man's face.

"You come to see me, mister?" the man asked.

"I did," Fargo said. "If you're the sheriff here."

"I am. Sheriff Al Johnson," the man said. "You wouldn't have been at Sam Whitford's place last night, would you, mister?"

"Just so happens I was," Fargo said. He heard the click of a hammer being drawn back, glanced to where the deputy held a six-gun trained on him. He looked back and saw the sheriff had pulled a Smith & Wesson Model I and leveled it at him. Fargo stared at the seven-shot, single-action weapon for a moment and returned his eyes to the bulbous-nosed face. "What the hell's this all about?" he growled.

"You're under arrest, mister," the sheriff said, "for the murder of Sam Whitford."

2

Fargo stared at Sheriff Johnson. "I didn't murder Sam Whitford. I found him dead. That's why I'm here," he protested.

"What's your name, mister?" the sheriff asked.

"Fargo . . . Skye Fargo. Some call me the Trailsman."

"You killed four of Hal Comager's boys, too," the sheriff said.

"You mean that posse of gunslingers. They started shooting before they reined up. I had to shoot back," Fargo said.

"That's not the way I heard it," Johnson said.

Fargo felt the anger balloon inside him. "I don't give a shit what you heard. That's the way it was," he snapped.

"Not according to Hal Comager," the sheriff said with dogged persistence.

"Who the hell's Hal Comager?" Fargo queried.

"Sam Whitford's foreman. It was Hal and his men who found you at the ranch," the sheriff said.

"He saw me outside. He didn't see me kill anybody. You can't arrest me on that."

"I'm not. I'm arrestin' you on Willie Magee's word. He said he saw you do it," Johnson answered.

"And who's Willie Magee?" Fargo frowned.

"A respected member of the community," the sheriff said. "He said he saw you murder Sam Whitford and his housemaid."

"That's a crock of shit. You're trying to set me up for this," Fargo barked.

"I'm just doing my job," the man said blandly.

"Well, you're doing it all wrong. This Willie Magee character saw somebody else, not me."

The sheriff shrugged. "You'll get your chance to tell your side of it to Judge Dorrance, soon as he gets back. Ought to be in a few days. Meanwhile, you're under arrest," he said.

Fargo's eyes flicked to the weapon in the sheriff's hand. The Smith & Wesson couldn't miss at that short distance, the Trailsman realized, and the deputy had him covered as well. The odds were definitely against him, and he didn't want to start by putting a bullet through the town sheriff. Not yet, anyway, he grunted silently.

"Something stinks here," he growled. "Maybe it's this Willie Magee. Maybe the foreman. Maybe they're in it together." He held back the other words that came to mind. Maybe you, too, he'd toyed with adding and decided against it for the moment.

"You'll have your day," Sheriff Johnson said,

and gestured to the deputy. "Take his gun, Herb," he said.

Fargo remained quiet as the deputy carefully stepped closer and lifted the Colt from its holster.

"Inside," the sheriff ordered, motioning to his office.

Johnson followed Fargo into a room that contained only a desk, a wall cabinet with a padlock on it, a file cabinet, and a wood desk chair. Past the room lay two small cells that were in view of anyone seated at the desk. Fargo felt the prod of a gun in his back. "The cell on the right," the sheriff said.

Fargo pulled the cell door open and stepped inside the stone-walled space. He saw a narrow cot, a washbasin, and a single barred window some six feet up from the floor.

He turned as the lock shut on the cell door. His lake-blue eyes were piercing as he gazed at Sheriff Johnson. "If I'd killed Sam Whitford, why would I come back to tell you about finding him?" he asked almost casually.

Sheriff Johnson let his lips purse for a moment. "I thought about that," he said, his shrewd eyes glinting. "You knew you'd been seen there. Maybe you figured this was a real smart move. Like you said, Hal and his boys had seen you, and nothing more. But you didn't know about Willie Magee."

"That's true," Fargo said. "And I didn't murder Sam Whitford either." He turned away, his mouth a thin line. The double-edged throwing knife lay in the calf-holster about his leg. He'd use it if he had to, but right now he was curious about what they'd do next. Patience might bring more answers than anything else for the moment. The sheriff hadn't asked him a damn question—what he claimed to be doing there, if he had a story of his own, not even where he'd come from. Was it because he didn't want to wrestle with his conscience if he heard anything that sounded reasonable? Or was it because he didn't give a damn about hearing anything else?

Fargo let the questions hang as he sat down on the edge of the cot. The sheriff put his Colt into the cabinet, and the deputy snapped to attention as the door opened and the hatchet-jawed man strode in.

Sheriff Johnson jerked a thumb toward the cell before the man said anything. "That him?" he asked, and Fargo saw the man's eyes widen as he stared into the cell.

"Jesus, you got him already," the man said, and Fargo rose to his feet and stepped to the bars.

"He came in with a story about finding Sam dead," the sheriff said. "Name's Skye Fargo."

"You must be Comager," Fargo muttered.

"Bastard. You cost me four good men," Hal Comager half-snarled.

"You cost yourself four men," Fargo returned.

"You'll hang for this," the man grated.

"Don't count on it," Fargo said calmly.

Comager's hatchet jaw thrust forward as he turned to the sheriff. "I wouldn't wait for the judge if it was me," he snapped.

"Now, Hal, we don't want to go lynchin' folks here. You know we've got him dead to rights. Judge Dorrance will know it, too," the sheriff said soothingly. "You just leave it to me, now."

Comager snorted but strode out of the office, and Fargo watched Sheriff Johnson turn to his deputy. "Get some rest. You take the night shift, Herb." The deputy nodded and walked from the office.

Fargo returned to the cot and stretched out, his eyes narrowed in thought, his long frame hanging over the end of the cot. The exchange between Hal Comager and Johnson had been interesting—Comager angry and nervous, the sheriff calm and soothing—not unlike two partners concerned about the same thing, each in their own way, Fargo found himself thinking. But it was still too early for conclusions, so he watched the sheriff fold himself into the chair at the desk and begin to shuffle through a drawer full of papers.

He let the man do his work for over an hour before he called out, "Where's my horse?"

"Public stable, not that you'll be needing him," the sheriff said.

"I just want to know he's being taken care of. He's a mighty fine horse," Fargo said.

"He seems that. You hadn't been riding such a specially marked horse maybe you wouldn't be here now," Sheriff Johnson said.

"Maybe," Fargo said, and fell silent. He allowed some more of the day to go on before he raised his voice again. "Sam Whitford have a lot of enemies?" he asked.

The sheriff gave a wry, snorting laugh. "You trying to find something to hang your hat on, boy?" he returned.

"Just curious," Fargo said.

"Every man's got enemies," the sheriff said. "I guess you were one of his."

Fargo smiled and let the remark go by. "This Willie Magee, was he at the party?" he asked, peering out at the sheriff.

"What party?" Johnson frowned.

"The one Sam Whitford had before he was murdered," Fargo snapped, and caught the moment of uncertainty in the sheriff's shrewd eyes. "Didn't you know he'd held a big party?" he pressed.

"Sure, sure I knew," the man said too quickly.

"Was Willie Magee a guest there?" Fargo pushed.

"More likely he was helping out," the sheriff answered with caution in his voice. "I wouldn't exactly know."

"How come Hal Comager happened to come by when I was there? Or wouldn't you exactly know that, either?" Fargo speared.

"Don't get smart with me, mister," the sheriff flared. "Willie Magee was running and met up with him."

"All nice and neat, isn't it?" Fargo smiled, drawing a glare from the sheriff, and he turned aside, closed his eyes, and let the hours wear on. Two things had become clear: he had arrived at Sam Whitford's house just a little too late to help the man, and just at the right time to become a convenient scapegoat for somebody. He half-dozed on the cot, waiting for nightfall before making a move to leave the jail cell. It might not be easy to bring about, he realized, but night would afford the only chance. He lay still, patient and quiet, and he had just stretched his long, powerful arms over his head when the door flew open. He looked through the bars to see a girl burst into the office.

Short-cut brown hair, a pugnaciously pretty face with a collection of freckles across the bridge of her nose, she was a small girl but with a rounded, firm figure. He saw high, full breasts push against a yellow shirt and a round rear fill the riding britches she wore. "Miss Bonnie, I'll be dammed," he heard Sheriff Johnson exclaim, surprise flooding the man's voice. "You've never visited before."

"No man has ever killed my grandpa before," the girl snapped. "I just heard. Where is he?"

Sheriff Johnson gestured to the cell, and Fargo swung long legs from the cot and rose to his feet as the girl strode to the bars. Her brown eyes were just a shade darker than the short-cut brown hair, and she had full lips and smooth, round cheeks. "Damn you, mister. Goddamn you," she hissed, and he heard her voice break and saw tears edge the rims of her eyes.

"You believe everything you hear?" Fargo said quietly.

The girl spun on the sheriff, a frown creasing her smooth, slightly rounded brow. "You got him dead to rights or not?" she demanded.

"We got him," the sheriff said.

"Tell me," Bonnie snapped.

"Got somebody saw him do it," the man answered.

"Who?" she pressed.

"Willie Magee," Johnson said after a moment's hesitation.

"Shit," the girl said. "Is that all?"

"Hal Comager saw him outside the ranch," the sheriff said. "His name's Skye Fargo."

The girl looked across at Fargo. "Damn, that's

27

not enough. Judge Dorrance bends over backward to be fair. He's not going to believe Willie Magee," she said.

"He'll believe him. Willie saw him do it," the sheriff said.

"He didn't see me do anything," Fargo interjected.

"I don't like it," the girl said harshly. "I don't want my grandpa's killer walking away."

"He won't," Al Johnson said.

"Maybe he's good at convincing. Maybe Judge Dorrance will believe him," Bonnie countered.

"No chance of that. Just leave it all to me." The sheriff spoke soothingly but received only a pugnacious glower in return, Fargo noted.

"I don't want him buying his way out, either," the girl snapped, and Fargo saw redness flood the sheriff's face.

"You watch your damn mouth, Bonnie Whitford," the sheriff barked. "You can just get your ass out of here, girl."

"My pleasure." Bonnie strode from the office, a rounded, angry figure whose short, quick steps echoed her bristling anger. She slammed the door behind her, and Sheriff Johnson slowly turned toward Fargo.

"I wouldn't say she has a lot of confidence in you, Sheriff," Fargo remarked.

"Shut your mouth, damn you," the man snarled, and drew his Smith & Wesson half out of its holster. Fargo let a slow smile cross his face. Johnson's lips twitched for a moment before he let the gun fall back into the holster.

"That's being smart," Fargo said.

"Sit down before I change my mind," the sheriff said, and returned to his desk. The smile still held on Fargo's lips as he stretched out on the cot. He was more valuable to the sheriff alive for now. He was plainly needed as Sam Whitford's killer, a criminal to be properly tried and hung for all to see. But Bonnie Whitford's words hung in his mind. She had all but said that bribery had been a part of the sheriff's career. It was another item he tucked away in his mind as he stretched out on the couch and gazed at the growing darkness outside. The sheriff lit a lamp atop the desk that sent weak flickers of light to the bars of the cell.

The front door opened and the deputy entered with a basket from which he drew a covered bowl and a piece of bread. At a nod from the sheriff, he brought the food to the cell, bent down, and slipped it through the space at the bottom of the bars. "Supper," he grunted.

Fargo brought the bowl back to the cot along with the piece of bread. He found a thick soup of uncertain ancestry, but he was hungry, he realized, and he'd eaten worse. He glanced up as the sheriff pulled the front door open.

"Don't take any chances with him, Herb," Sheriff Johnson told his deputy, and Herb nodded gravely. Fargo half-smiled as he finished his bread and the sheriff left. He put the dish down and relaxed on the cot as night grew deeper. When midnight neared, he reached down and drew the double-edged blade from the calf holster around his leg. Holding the thin knife up the sleeve of his shirt, he rose and lifted the soup bowl with his other hand.

"You want to take this out of here?" he called, and stepped to the cell bars.

The deputy dropped his feet down from the desk and started toward him. Fargo's muscles tensed as he readied himself to snap one hand through the space between the bars and grab the deputy's shirt while holding the blade into his ribs with the other. But the man halted a half-dozen feet from the bars, suddenly growing wary.

"Put it down and step back," Herb said, and Fargo swore under his breath. He lowered the bowl to the space at the bottom of the bars and took a step backward. But the deputy didn't move. "All the way back."

The Trailsman muttered an oath under his breath as he stepped back farther. The deputy carefully approached the cell, one eye on the big man inside it. His hand rested on his six-gun as he bent down and pulled the bowl out. Fargo lowered himself onto the cot. He felt the frustration spiraling inside him, but he let another hour go by before he called out again.

"I'm thirsty, dammit. It's not right to keep a man in here without water."

"I'll get you some water. Shut up," the deputy growled. He loped from behind the desk and went to a pitcher in one corner of the office, filled a glass, and started toward the cell. Fargo approached the bars, muscles tensed, the knifeblade concealed in the right sleeve of his shirt, ready to drop instantly into his palm. But Herb halted again before reaching the bars. "Back," he ordered. "All the way back." Fargo swore inwardly again, though he shrugged and moved away. The man put the glass down at the bottom of the cell door and quickly retreated.

Fargo walked forward, pulled the glass through, and drank, more to carry through the tiny charade than from thirst. He carried the half-emptied glass back to the cot with him, his lips a thin line. Once again he waited, not more than a half-hour this time, before rising to his feet again. "How about a smoke?" he asked from the bars of the cell door.

"You're gettin' to be a pain in the ass," Herb spit out, but he rose and started toward the cell. Halfway there, he halted and tossed a rolled cigarette through the bars, followed by a wooden match. "Have your smoke, and go to sleep and shut up," the man snapped, and turned back to the desk.

Fargo retrieved the cigarette and the match, keeping an eye on Herb, who was leaning his head back against the wall and closing his eyes. Fargo sat down on the edge of the cot and swore silently again. His plans had taken an unexpected turn. He hadn't thought the deputy would be that careful—or cagey, he grunted. The throwing knife slid from his sleeve to his palm, and he turned the thin blade in his hand. It would be simple enough to send the blade hurtling between the bars and into the man's chest. That would leave the deputy very dead . . . but with the keys to the cell very out of reach, Fargo realized. Damn, he murmured, and lay back on the cot as he searched his mind for a way to bring the deputy within reach. But as the time ticked away, he found himself unable to think of anything that wasn't a variation on what he'd already tried, and Herb wasn't about to fall for those ruses.

Fargo's lips pulled back in a grimace as he thought

about trying to stage a fake stomachache or even a cataleptic fit. But he discarded the thought as too transparent. He had begun to search again when he heard the faint sound, a softly scraping noise. He glanced at the deputy, but the man remained asleep, head against the wall. The sound came again and Fargo swung from the cot, frowning as he listened, then spinning on silent, catlike steps to peer at the barred window. He moved forward and saw the length of string being lowered along the inside wall from the window, a six-gun tied to the end of it. He reached out, closed one hand around the gun, and saw the folded piece of paper stuck between the hammer and the chamber.

He also saw the string go slack and tumble to the ground the moment he grabbed the gun. He peered up at the barred window, his ears straining, and caught the sound of footsteps hurrying away in the darkness outside. He dropped to one knee as he extracted the slip of paper from the gun, unfolded it, and peered at the words printed in large, block letters.

RIDE SOUTH ON ROAD. TAKE LEFT
AT TALL ROCK. GO UP HILL TO LAKE.

He read the instructions twice before he tore the note into shreds, stood on tiptoe, and let it blow out of the barred window. He checked the chamber of the gun, a Remington-Beals pocket revolver, five-shot, single-action, with a brass trigger guard, and found the five chambers filled. He moved to the bars of the cell and, holding the gun behind him, snapped words out. "Wake up, stupid," he barked. The deputy's eyes flickered open. "I need you over here," Fargo said.

Herb rose, came halfway across the floor toward him, and halted. "Well, you're not getting me over there. You got something to say you better say it now," he said.

Fargo's hand pushed halfway through the bars, the gun aimed directly at the deputy's chest. The man's eyes grew wide in surprise that instantly turned to fear.

"One wrong move and I blow you apart," Fargo said, and Herb remained still, his eyes on the revolver. "Take your gun out and drop it on the floor, nice and slow," Fargo ordered, and the deputy obeyed. "Now come over here and toss your keys in," Fargo said, and again Herb did as he was told, his eyes almost riveted on the gun. The jailhouse keys landed on the floor inside the cell, and Fargo kept the gun trained on the deputy as he bent down and scooped up the keys with his other hand. "Come over here to the bars." The man obeyed. "Now turn around," Fargo said, and heard the quaver in Herb's voice.

"You wouldn't shoot a man in the back, would you?" the deputy whined.

"Never," Fargo said as he brought the gun down on the man's head. Herb collapsed at once and Fargo reached through the bars, put the key into the lock from outside, and clicked the cell door open. He stepped outside, pausing only to push the deputy's body into the cell and lock the door. He tossed the keys into a corner of the office, then went to the cabinet and retrieved his Colt before hurrying from the jailhouse. Outside, the night deep and dark, he strode to the public stable only a street away and asked for the Ovaro. The stable boy hesitated but quickly thought better of it and brought the horse to him saddled and ready to ride. Fargo took the pinto through the silent streets of Horsehead, riding south as his thoughts raced in time with the hoofbeats of the horse.

He had no friends in this part of the country, but it seemed as though Sam Whitford did, Fargo mused. He guessed he'd been riding for about fifteen minutes when he saw the tall rock standing like a lone sentinel. He turned left and began to climb a low hillside of hawthorn. When the land leveled, he caught sight of the last of the moonlight glinting on a small lake. He slowed the Ovaro to a trot, drawing closer to the water, then brought the horse to a walk. The moon had begun to dip below the distant horizon as Fargo scanned the night darkness. But no one moved from the trees to meet him, so he moved even closer to the lake, the hairs along the back of his neck beginning to rise. Still no one appeared from the darkness, but the sixth sense he'd long ago learned to trust was suddenly spearing him.

He reined up sharply, hunched low in the saddle, and let the silence engulf him. He was almost at the water's edge when he caught the sound, the faint, rustling sound of a heavy branch being pushed aside. He dived from the saddle as the shot rang out, the heavy report of a rifle, a shot that would have slammed into him were he still on the horse. But he was on the ground, landing on his shoulder and flipping himself over as another shot rang out, this time plowing into the ground nearby. Fargo saw the water only a half-dozen feet away, rolled again as a third shot barely missed him, came up on his feet, and dodged to his left as yet another shot whistled by. He swerved sharp right then leapt into the water headfirst. He struck out for deeper water at once and two more shots hit the surface, this time from a six-gun. Another brace of shots kicked up spray only inches from him, and he knew turning and drawing his own gun would be a fatal mistake. Another shot sent up a small geyser of water only a fraction of an inch from his face.

He let out a groan, threw one arm into the air, and let himself go under the surface. He stayed down until his lungs began to burn then he slowly floated up. He kept his body limp, arms and legs spread out as he surfaced. But he held his head sideways so he could take a quick gulp of air as he lay limply atop the lake. The water began to push him the few feet toward the shore, but he remained limp and spread-eagled. Through eyes that were only slits, he peered across the surface of the lake and saw the small form standing at the edge of the shore. A flash of short brown hair gave him a hard jab of surprise. He floated onto the soft sand at the edge of the lake and lay still, a seemingly lifeless form. The movement of the water pushed his body sideways and he saw, through his half-turned face, the figure of the girl step closer to stand in the water as she stared down at him.

Her arms hung straight down along her sides, the six-gun held loosely in one hand, he noted. "Dammit, you deserve it for what you did," Fargo heard her say, though she sounded as if she were trying hard to convince herself. "Why'd you do it, damn you? Why?" she went on, and he caught the sob in her voice. "You had no right, no damn right," she said. "At least now you won't buy off Johnson or sweet-talk the judge."

Fargo stayed limp and let the water push his outspread arms closer to her. His right hand brushed against her ankle, but she didn't move, still staring down at him. The gun hung loosely in her hand. Fargo tensed his muscles, let another few seconds go by, and shot his arm out with the speed of a rattler's strike. His hand came around behind her ankle; he pulled and she went down hard on her back. Shallow water sprayed upward and she let out a gasp of surprise. Fargo half-rose, dived across her, and closed one hand around her wrist. He twisted and the gun fell from her hand, but he felt her legs come up. He managed to turn himself in time to take the kick against the muscled side of his right thigh.

"Bastard," she screamed, and tried to rake her nails down his face. He pulled back and she managed to twist her wrist free, rolled, and tried to scramble away. But he dived forward, caught her around the legs, and brought her down, his face coming down against a round, soft rear. He lifted her, turned her around, and tossed her down hard on her back, and he heard the breath rush from her.

"That's all, goddammit," he roared. "Crazy little hell-fire, aren't you?" Her answer was to try another kick at his groin, but he turned away in time to slam her down onto the ground again as she tried to rise. Again, he heard the breath rush from her, but she lifted herself up onto her elbows and her brown eyes shot fire at him.

"All right, go on, kill me too," she half-shouted, her breasts pressed up tight against the dampness of her shirt, her short hair falling over her forehead.

"I didn't kill your grandpa, dammit," Fargo threw back.

"They say Willie Magee saw you do it," Bonnie Whitford snapped.

"He lied. You said yourself he wasn't a man the judge would be quick to believe," Fargo returned.

"I know what I said," the girl answered truculently.

"I didn't kill Sam Whitford," Fargo said again.

Bonnie peered hard at him and brushed the medium-brown hair from her forehead. "Words. Denying's easy."

"So's accusing," Fargo countered.

"You were there, Hal Comager found you there," Bonnie Whitford flared.

"Yes, I was there. Your grandpa hired me and I'd just arrived. That's when I found him and the housemaid," Fargo said.

"Agnes Pilford," Bonnie muttered. "Been with Grandpa for ten years." He let her push herself to her feet and she continued to stare angrily at him.

"Ever hear of jumping to conclusions?" Fargo asked her.

Her pert face glowered as she studied him again. "Why'd my grandpa hire you?" she asked.

"I don't know," Fargo said.

She uttered a snorting sound. "Isn't that convenient?"

"He was going to tell me when I got here," Fargo said.

"You really expect me to believe that?" Bonnie Whitford flung back.

"It's the truth, whether you believe it or not. He hired me back in Independence Rock two months ago."

Her smooth, round forehead crinkled with a frown. "He did go there two months ago," she murmured.

"If I'd killed him, why didn't I just hightail it when I got out of the sheriff's jailhouse? Why did I bother coming here?"

"Maybe you thought it was smarter to find out who got you out first," she answered.

He took in her rage, suspicion fed by a terrible fury, fury by a consuming hurt. He had to find a way to reach her, to break through her righteous anger. She was important, perhaps the only avenue to uncovering the truth. But to reach her he'd have to do something bold, something to shatter her seething certainty. "You don't want your grandpa's killer to get away," he said.

"You're damn right," she flung back.

"You went to a lot of trouble to make sure of that," Fargo said. She glared back at him, defiantly determined. He lifted the Colt from its holster and held it out to her. Surprise flooded her face. "Go on, now's your chance. Take it and finish what you started," he said.

She stared at him, but then she took the gun and turned it on him instantly. He wondered if boldness was about to backfire. Then she hesitated, still staring.

"What are you waiting for if you're so sure?" Fargo prodded. "You almost blew my head off without a question. Now's your chance to make the same mistake twice."

The frown wrinkled itself into her smooth forehead. She blinked. He saw her throat move as she swallowed hard. Slowly, she lowered the gun to stand silently in front of him, tears edging her eyes.

But her lips remained tight and angry, forming the incongruous picture of a belligerent waif. He reached down and gently took the gun from her hand.

"You must have cared very much for him," Fargo said quietly.

"Yes," she said, her eyes soft for a moment. "He raised me, from when I was a little girl. He always understood me, always was there for me." She halted and peered at the gun Fargo held loosely in his hand, lifted her eyes to search his chiseled handsomeness. "I was wrong about you," she murmured.

"You were," Fargo said.

She blinked again. "I guess I've been real dumb. Or maybe a little out of my mind. I wanted to strike back at someone."

"And there I was, accused and jailed," Fargo said.

She groaned and looked away. "Oh, God, I'm so glad I missed," she said. She brought her eyes back to him. "I'm sorry. I know that's not saying much, but I don't have anything else to say."

"That'll have to do, then," Fargo said. "But you and I might have a lot to talk about."

"Come to my place. You can stay there. Sheriff Johnson will be out looking for you. He certainly won't look at my place," Bonnie Whitford said.

"I'd guess not," Fargo agreed.

Bonnie walked to her horse, the damp shirt clinging to the round, high breasts to outline each lovely shape. He climbed onto the Ovaro and swung in beside her as the pink grayness of dawn began to slide across the sky. She cut through the hawthorns and rode north, emerging in a long, wide valley that finally led to a modest wood-frame ranch house with a half-dozen corrals spilling out from the rear. He followed Bonnie to a stable with a roan in one stall, and she gestured to the corner stall. He stabled the Ovaro, unsaddled the horse, and went with her through a passage that connected to a side door of the house. She lifted a lamp, though dawn was starting to seep into the house. The living room was modestly furnished, a coffee table nearly hidden by books on breeding and animal care, and a pair of deep, stuffed chairs. Two doors led to adjoining rooms at the rear of the room.

Bonnie Whitford turned to him, her pert face suddenly drawn and haggard. "Talking will have to wait. I'm just wrung out. I'm sick, hurt, and emptied. There's an extra room in the back. Nothing fancy, but it has a real bed and it's warm and dry," she said.

"Sounds just fine," Fargo told her.

She paused, brown eyes grave. Again she was a conflicting mixture of pugnaciousness and vulnerability. "Stay and help me, Fargo," she said. "Somebody killed my grandpa. I'm going to find out who."

"We'll talk later," he said. "Get some sleep now."

She nodded gravely and walked from the room.

He crossed to the doorway she had indicated to a neat, square room with a single window and a wide bed. As he pulled off clothes, the weariness pulled on him. He stretched out on the bed, enjoying the luxury of the soft mattress, and fell asleep at once.

3

Sun filled the room as Fargo stretched, rose, and went to the window to see the orange sphere hanging in the noonday sky. He pulled on trousers and went outside to the well, drew a bucket of water, and washed. When he finished, he leaned against the house and let the warm sun dry his muscled torso and strong, chiseled face. He closed his eyes, face turned up, and snapped them open when he heard the sound at the doorway, the rustle of fabric. Bonnie was standing there, her glance taking in the beauty of his half-naked body.

She was dressed and scrubbed, her pert face almost shining, the line of freckles across her nose accented in the bright sun. She was uncommonly pretty, he decided, her determined pugnaciousness giving a special vibrancy to her prettiness.

"I made breakfast. More like lunch, now," she said. "Biscuits, jam and coffee."

"Be right in," Fargo said as he hurried into the

house to finish dressing. He found her in a small kitchen with a puncheon table, tin plates, and wood utensils. He sat and gazed at her round, firm loveliness, high breasts pressing against the light-blue cotton blouse as she served him, her legs round and full inside the riding britches. The biscuits were tasty and the coffee strong and good. She sat down across from him, all pert and high-spirited determination now.

"Will you stay and help me, Fargo?" she asked. "I'm going to find who killed my grandpa."

"How?" he asked with a smile.

"I don't know, but I'll do it," she said with a rush of confidence. "It won't be easy, I know that, but dammit, I'll do it." She paused and tightened her lips. "All right, I'll need help. I'll need you," she said.

"Never went from suspect to savior overnight," Fargo remarked.

"There's a first time for everything," Bonnie said. "I've saved some money. I'll pay you all I can."

"No need for that," Fargo said. She frowned, but he continued. "Sam Whitford paid me to come here. I figure I owe him for that. I owe it to myself to stay, too," he said with honesty. "The sheriff still has me marked for a murderer. But I have some questions. Let's start with your grandpa first. Tell me about him."

She rose and started to clear the table as she answered. "To me, he was the most wonderful person in the world. As I told you, he raised me. My ma and pa were killed when I was hardly five. I don't remember much about either of them. I was a problem, I know—never liked schooling, never took to the foolish ways of most girls, never made many friends. But Grandpa always understood when nobody else did. He never gave in to me, but he understood and that was important."

"No boyfriends now? You're a right pretty thing," Fargo said.

She wrinkled her nose and the freckles seemed to dance. "There've been a few. Couldn't take any for long. Some tried too hard, some not enough," she said.

"I can understand that." Fargo's laughter drew an instant glower from Bonnie.

"What's that supposed to mean?" she snapped.

"I imagine you'd be a damn hard package to handle for most young fellers," Fargo said.

She sniffed at his answer and frowned back. "Why'd you ask about boyfriends, anyway?"

"I wondered if there was anybody Sam Whitford threw out who might have come back for revenge," Fargo answered.

"No, nothing like that. I did all my own throwing out," Bonnie said. "And none of it recent. We can talk more while I feed," she said, and started for the door.

He followed her outside, helped her carry feed pails into the first corral, and found himself surrounded by a collection of dense-coated, black-and-white sheep that pushed and rubbed against him as Bonnie filled their feed bins. He ran his fingers over the coat of one young ewe and saw she had a double coat, the outer one coarse to the touch, the inner one downy soft.

"Navajo-Churra sheep," Bonnie said. "Real hardy and real easy to handle. Much better than Dorset or Suffolk, I think."

He followed her into the next corral, which contained a half-dozen hogs, one a huge sow with a litter of piglets. All had reddish skin and snouts considerably longer and thinner than any hogs he'd ever seen.

"Tamworth," Bonnie said. "Strong, hardy, with a skin pigmentation that protects them from the sun. I'll take them over Poland China or Berkshire any day, which is what most folks breed around here." She finished filling the feed bins, set down the pails, and straightened up, arching herself backward as she stretched.

Fargo watched the high, round breasts press hard against the shirt without the trace of a tiny point showing. Bonnie was all pert roundness, he decided, her edges all of the spirit rather than the body.

"I'm going to start raising some Gloucester and Belted Galloway herds one day," she said. "Soon as I can get more time and some good starting animals. Everybody else has Herefords and Holsteins around here."

"And you don't do what everybody else does," Fargo prodded.

"I think it's important these breeds stay alive and healthy," Bonnie said. "They have qualities the others don't. Everybody starts raising one kind of hog or one kind of sheep or cattle, and sooner or later they'll be in trouble. Something goes wrong with their strain, they'll have nothing to fall back on. That's another thing Grandpa understood. He listened to me and told me do the things I think are important. That's why he was so special to me."

"Somebody didn't like him," Fargo said quietly, and saw the anger instantly rise in her face.

"Somebody I'm going to find," she said harshly before stalking out of the corral. He followed her. She halted in front of the house and turned to him. "I'm sorry. I shouldn't flare up like that."

"A fire sends out sparks," Fargo said, and she smiled. It was the first time he'd seen her smile, he realized, and it added to her pert prettiness, the small, pug nose crinkling up and the freckles dancing again. "Sam Whitford ever tell you about business problems? Ever mention anybody he was having trouble with?" Fargo asked.

"No. He kept the other part of his life to himself. We had our world, he and I. That was enough for me. But once a month he'd go away, regular as clockwork. Business, he said, but he never told me another thing about it." She fell silent and walked with him as he went into the stable and began to saddle the Ovaro. "The funeral's tomorrow," she said. "I arranged that with Seth Owens, the undertaker, first thing after I learned what happened."

"Before you stormed into the jail?" Fargo smiled. She nodded. "You expect a crowd?" he asked.

"Some." She shrugged. "Some will come because they're really grieving, most because they think it's the proper thing to do."

"I think I ought to be there," Fargo said. "Sometimes you learn things at funny places."

"Knob Hill, west of town," Bonnie said.

"Your grandpa had a fancy party night before last. Were you there?" Fargo asked.

"No. I hardly ever went to those things."

"You know who was there?" Fargo questioned.

"I know who he invited," Bonnie said, and frowned at him. "You think it was somebody who was at the party?"

45

"Can't rule it out. Somebody could've left and come back, knowing he'd be alone. The maid just got in the way," Fargo answered. "You can give me the list later. Right now I want to pay a visit to this Willie Magee. Where'll I find him?"

"Either at the bar at Carrie's bunkhouse, or at that shack of his," Bonnie said.

Fargo frowned. "The sheriff said he was a respected town citizen."

"Hah!" Bonnie snorted. "He's the town drunk. He'd do or say anything for a fifty-cent gold piece or a full bottle."

"Then I have some hard questions for Mr. Magee," Fargo said. "I'll try Carrie's bunkhouse first."

"I'll go to his shack. It's just outside the south end of town. If he's there, I'll see that he stays there," Bonnie said.

"No sense in sticking your neck out," Fargo told her.

Her jaw thrust forward. "I need your help, but I won't sit by," she said.

"Guess not." Fargo chuckled. "That wouldn't be your way." He turned and climbed onto the Ovaro.

"Be careful. Sheriff Johnson's looking for you, remember," Bonnie said.

"You don't think much of the sheriff, do you?" Fargo commented.

"That weasel," Bonnie snapped. "He's made a career of letting prisoners buy their way out."

"You the only one who knows that?" Fargo queried.

"No, but nobody ever did anything about it. Never was able to understand that," she said.

"See you later, one place or another," Fargo said, and she nodded.

He rode from the modest ranch, glanced back to see her watch him go, then he turned the horse south and started toward the town. The sun had begun to slide into the late-afternoon sky when he neared Horsehead. He made a circle that brought him along the back edge of the town. He rode slowly behind the buildings as the shadows lengthened. When he reached the rear of the dance hall, he turned into a narrow alleyway alongside the building. He tethered the Ovaro close to the wall and walked to the main street, halting as he saw the deputy, Herb, ride by on a brown mare. Fargo waited until well after the man had gone before he stepped into the street and strode to the dance hall.

It was already crowded, a line of drinkers along the bar and many of the round tables taken. He saw the girls in low-cut, cheap, tight dresses moving among the customers, some definitely pairing off, others waiting. He continued to scan the room until he spotted the woman at one corner of the bar. A red satin dress two sizes too small encased a full-busted figure with the tightness of a second skin. Bottle blond hair and too much powder and paint made guessing her age an uncertain venture—somewhere between thirty and forty, he decided—but behind all the excesses he saw an attractive face, strong features, a wide, warm mouth despite too much lipstick, dark-blue eyes, the face of a woman who had seen the worst in human behavior but had managed to avoid a harsh bitterness. Her eyes locked with his as he made his way across the room to her.

"Hello, big man," she said in a throaty tone, instant interest flickering in her eyes.

"You Carrie?" Fargo asked.

"Bull's-eye," the woman said. "But then you figured that, didn't you?" she added with an appraising look.

"I did." Fargo smiled. "I thought you could point out Willie Magee to me. Heard he spends a good part of his time here."

"He does, but he left about an hour ago," Carrie said. "Willie Magee's getting awful popular suddenly."

Fargo felt the stab of apprehension go through him instantly. "Meaning what exactly?"

"Somebody was in here before asking for him," Carrie said.

"Who?" Fargo asked.

"Didn't know him," she said.

"When?" Fargo questioned sharply.

"Maybe ten, fifteen minutes back," the woman said.

"Obliged," Fargo said, and spun on his heel.

"Come back," he heard Carrie call as he crossed the room as fast as the crowd would allow. He leapt onto the Ovaro, skirted a heavy dray with chain-linked stakes, swerved around a buckboard driven by an elderly lady in her town finery, and sent the horse racing to the end of town. When he reached it, he saw the shack a few hundred yards away, two horses outside it, one the roan he'd seen in Bonnie's stable. He charged forward, cursing the sinking feeling in his stomach. He leapt from the saddle before the horse came to a halt. He pounded into the shack and heard the voices, one Bonnie's, the other a man's voice.

"Bastard," he heard Bonnie curse as he pushed through a collection of boxes and cartons piled almost to the ceiling and came onto a small back room in the shack. The man had both of Bonnie's wrists twisted behind her back, and he moved his legs to one side to avoid the backward kicks she aimed at him.

"Real little hellion, aren't you?" the man growled. "Well, you need a little taming, sweetie."

Fargo took another moment to see the figure crumpled facedown on the ground, a red stain seeping across the half-rotted floorboards of the shack. He drew the Colt and stepped from the welter of boxes.

"Let her go, mister."

The man froze for a moment to stare at him. But the moment ended and he yanked the girl in front of him and drew his six-gun. Fargo flung himself to the side, crashed into the pile of boxes and cartons as two shots flew past him. He half-fell, half-rolled as another two shots sent a cascade of wood and cardboard into the air. On his stomach behind a tall crate, he saw the man still holding Bonnie in front of him, his gun hand held around her, ready to fire again. The man started to edge across the floor, keeping Bonnie tight against him as a shield. Fargo swore silently. He couldn't risk a shot, not with the man moving through the half-light of the shack. He had to get him to stand still. Thumb on the hammer, he squinted, aimed and raised his voice. "You hurt her and you're a dead man," he called.

"You try anything and she's a dead cookie," the man answered, still sliding his way past boxes toward the door of the shack.

Fargo tried to draw a bead on his head, but the man pulled Bonnie in front of the sight he had taken. Fargo moved along the other side of the mountain of boxes, parallel to the man. He'd have to swing around when he reached the door, so Fargo crept sideways, halted, and took aim again as the man reached the half-open door. But he didn't swing around to drag Bonnie outside with him. He halted, instead, keeping the girl hard against him. "Throw your gun out," the man called.

Fargo swore silently and remained motionless behind the boxes. A little piece of the man's head afforded the only meager target as it protruded to one side behind Bonnie's short, brown hair. Fargo raised the Colt, but the man moved and the target vanished.

"Throw it out or I'll put a bullet through her head," the man threatened, and pressed the gun against Bonnie's temple. He was smart and desperate and Fargo held no illusions about him. He'd keep hold of Bonnie only until he felt secure enough to kill her and toss her aside. But Fargo knew he had only two bullets left in the gun. His thoughts raced.

"All right, you win," he called out. He threw the Colt in an arc, but only far enough for it to land just on the other side of the boxes. Instantly, he whipped the thin-bladed throwing knife from the calf holster around his leg. It was raised, ready to throw before the Colt stopped sliding along the floor. He waited, jaw muscles throbbing, eyes on the man at the doorway. Go for it, damn you, Fargo urged silently, his hand tight around the hilt of the knife.

The man waited, plainly wrestling with the thought. As Fargo cursed inwardly, the man backed to the doorway with Bonnie. Fargo smashed his fist into one of the boxes and the entire pyramid toppled. The man fired instantly, the bullet hurtling through the boxes, but Fargo stayed low. The man yanked Bonnie through the doorway with him. Fargo leapt to his feet and raced forward, knocking boxes aside on the way. The man had one bullet left . . .

Fargo scooped up the Colt as he crossed the room in a driving stride. He dropped to one knee when he reached the doorway and saw the man atop his horse with Bonnie, the gun held to her temple.

"Come out, damn you," the man ordered. "Come out with your hands up."

Fargo swore again. If he came out, he'd be a perfect target for the man's last bullet. If he didn't, the man was nervous enough and desperate enough to race off with Bonnie, shoot her, and toss her away as he took off. But he was also nervous enough to panic, his reactions instant and undisciplined. He'd shown that much when he shot at the boxes.

Fargo peered at Bonnie, the revolver against her temple. There was fear in her face, but it was mixed with an anger that made her brown eyes shoot dark fires and the pug nose tilt even further upward. He had to take the chance. Anything less would seal her fate as well as his.

"You got one second more or I blow her away," the man called, nervousness in his voice.

Fargo rose into a half-crouch, gathering powerful calf and thigh muscles. Colt in hand, finger against the trigger, he realized that he was really banking on the man's jittery nerves. He drew a deep breath and, with a roar, flung himself through the doorway in a diving leap. He landed outside on one shoulder, rolled, and twisted to one side. But the man's curse and the gunshot came together, and Fargo felt the bullet slam into the ground at least an inch away from him.

"Goddamn," the man swore again as Fargo came up on one knee. With a backhand motion, he sent Bonnie flying from the saddle and spurred the horse into a gallop at the same time. But Fargo, on one knee, had the Colt raised. The man tried to flatten himself on the horse's back, but Fargo fired, two shots, and the fleeing rider bucked in the saddle as though he'd suddenly been caught in a giant convulsion. The horse literally ran out from under him and he landed facedown in the dirt, an inert, silent form.

Fargo rose and strode to where Bonnie pushed herself up. She fell against him, high, round breasts warm as they pressed into his chest. He held her with one hand against her firm back. It had worked, he sighed. The man had followed his uncontrolled reactions—to his own death.

Bonnie finally pushed away, her eyes grave. "I'm owing you, Fargo. I won't forget it," she said in a level tone. "I was scared, I don't mind saying."

"What happened?" Fargo questioned.

"He'd just killed Willie Magee when I came in," she said. "He came at me, of course. Then you showed up, thank God."

Fargo glanced at the man's crumpled form. "You ever see him before?" he asked.

"Don't know his name, but he worked for Simon Carter," Bonnie said.

"Who's that?" Fargo queried.

"One of Grandpa's friends. Head of a mining operation west of town," Bonnie said. "He was at the party."

Fargo felt his brow crease as he pondered her words. He walked to the dead man, turned him over, and went through his pockets. Around his waist, the man wore a leather coin pouch; Fargo opened it and extracted a roll of bills. He counted a hundred dollars and pushed the money back in the pouch.

"Seems as though he'd been well paid to get rid of Willie Magee," Fargo said. Going through the man's hip pocket he found a receipt for repairs to a saddle. "His name was Elwood Cord," Fargo said, and walked to the man's horse. "Nothing," he grunted as he inspected the horse. "He was paid, but he wasn't ready to hightail it yet."

"How do you know that?" Bonnie asked.

"A man running takes his gear with him. There's not even a poncho on his horse, to say nothing of a bedroll or traveling blankets," Fargo said.

"Maybe he wasn't going to run," Bonnie ventured.

"Man does this kind of job, he usually heads for faraway places," Fargo said. "Seems to me this Simon Carter needs a visit. I'll go alone. You wait for me at your place. We'll talk when I get back. There are a lot of things that point the wrong way."

She nodded and climbed onto her horse. The Trailsman waited until she was out of sight before he climbed onto the pinto. He had a stop to make before visiting Simon Carter.

He rode back to Horsehead, unhurriedly made his way through town, and reined up before the sheriff's office, where the deputy's jaw hung open in astonishment as he stared up at him.

"Sheriff," Herb called out in a strangulated voice.

Fargo had his hand resting on the butt of the Colt as Sheriff Johnson emerged from the office to also stare at him in surprise.

"Goddamn, you've got your brass, I'll give you that," Sheriff Johnson breathed.

"No brass. Just pure in heart," Fargo said. "I didn't kill Sam Whitford and Willie Magee won't be accusing me of it."

"Why not?" Johnson asked.

"Willie Magee's dead," Fargo said.

"Shit," the man breathed as he frowned at Fargo. "And maybe you killed him."

"Feller by the name of Elwood Cord killed him," Fargo said.

"Why the hell should I believe that?" Johnson barked.

"Because Bonnie Whitford saw him do it," Fargo said, and drew another hiss of surprise from the man. "Just thought I'd stop by and tell you that," Fargo said. "And one thing more."

"What's that?" Johnson glowered.

"I'm going to find Sam Whitford's killer," Fargo said. "Don't get in my way."

"You threatenin' me?" the sheriff blustered.

"Wouldn't think of it. Just handing out friendly advice." Fargo smiled. He turned the Ovaro and halted as the sheriff called after him.

"Bustin' out of jail's an offense. I could arrest you for that," the man said.

Fargo let his eyes go to a small wooden knot at the top of one end of the hitching post. With the speed of a diamondback's strike, he drew the Colt and fired and the knot disappeared in a shower of wood splinters. He returned his eyes to the sheriff as the man stared at the single splinter of wood remaining atop the hitching post.

"You mean you could try, don't you?" Fargo said pleasantly. He laughed as he holstered the Colt and rode away.

Sheriff Johnson was a small-time opportunist. Bonnie's remarks about the man were enough to fix him as that. It wasn't likely that he'd murdered Sam Whitford, but he could be part of something bigger, Fargo thought as he rode west along a gravelly path that turned northwest after a few miles. He was about to turn off and try another direction when the barren hills rose up ahead of him. He spurred the horse on.

The hills quickly took the shape of shale-mining formations, figures and mining carts looking like tiny toys against the gray earth. He saw the house a few hundred yards to the right and turned toward it. A stone base with a log exterior, the house was large and sturdy, with big bay windows that looked out across a half-dozen small huts and a long bunkhouse. A man stepped from the house as Fargo dismounted, tall, thin, with a dour expression and watery blue eyes. He wore black trousers, a black vest with a gold watch chain hanging from one pocket and a white shirt.

"Looking for Simon Carter," Fargo said.

"I'm Simon Carter," the man answered.

"Got some questions for you," Fargo said. "Bonnie Whitford sent me." It was not exactly an untruth, he told himself. "Name's Fargo . . . Skye Fargo."

"Come in, Mr. Fargo." He followed Carter's thin figure into a richly furnished house with tall Oriental vases decorating every corner of a large living room. "Terrible thing about Sam, absolutely terrible," the man said solicitously.

"Wasn't it?" Fargo said. "Got some questions about Elwood Cord for you."

Simon Carter used his dour expression as a mask. "I don't know any Elwood Cord."

55

"Funny. I was told he worked for you," Fargo said blandly.

"You were told wrong," Simon countered. His voice was firm, but Fargo noted the tightness of his fingers that curled around the back of a chair.

"Too bad," Fargo said, and let his lips purse. "I get awful mean when I'm lied to."

Simon Carter's dour expression remained unchanged. "If that's all, please excuse me, Mr. Fargo. I've a lot of bookkeeping to finish," the man said.

The man was masking nervousness, Fargo decided, and thought about pressing further when the woman came into the room on quick steps through a side door, small, gray-haired, a tight face with a high-buttoned blouse and floor-length skirt.

"I've cleaned up all his things, Simon," she said, and halted abruptly, startled, when she saw Fargo to one side. "Oh, I'm sorry, Simon. I didn't see you had company."

"My wife, Ada," Simon Carter muttered.

Under his surface control the man was tense, and there was something flighty about Ada Carter. Fargo decided to press harder and skip politeness. "Whose things, ma'am?" he barked, and saw the woman grow flustered at once.

"Why, a . . . a man, a friend . . ." she stammered.

"My cousin's things," Simon Carter cut in sharply. "He was visiting and Ada just cleaned up the guest room." Fargo caught the quick glance he threw at his wife and the woman fell silent, her lips pressed together. But in her eyes Fargo saw instant nervousness.

"I think you can leave now, Mr. Fargo," Simon Carter said with a harsh stare.

"Why not?" Fargo smiled affably. "Thanks for your time."

Simon Carter hardly nodded and his face seemed to grow even more dour.

Fargo walked from the house, climbed onto the Ovaro, and slowly began to ride away. He threw a quick glance back and saw Simon Carter and his wife at the window, watching him go. Fargo urged the pinto into a trot. Something was very wrong. He'd been lied to by Simon Carter, he was certain. When he rode out of sight of the house, he swerved into the trees. He moved up a low hill and made a half-circle that brought him around to the side of the house still inside the trees. Carefully, he edged the horse downward until he reached the last of the trees, then he halted and swung to the ground. Four sheds of varying sizes dotted the open land, with the long bunkhouse stretching to the rear of the main house.

Dropping into a crouch, the Trailsman moved into the open land, darted forward to the nearest tool shed, and halted, his gaze on the main house. When he saw no one at the windows, he darted forward again, came up against another of the huts. He scanned the house once more. This time, from where he rested, he saw the wine-colored pony wagon at the rear of the house, harnessed to a brown horse, a quilting basket on the single seat. It was a wagon ready to roll. He waited a moment longer and scanned the shale hills to the sides. A half-dozen figures started walking down the nearest hill, another three riding along the bottom of the adjoining hill, all carrying their tools. But they were still a good distance away. Fargo rose, raced into the open again and reached the long bunkhouse. He pushed the door open and halted, let his eyes sweep the double rows of bunks that filled the long interior.

Some were half-made, most not, but a collection of personal gear was strewn near, on and half under each bunk. All except one, Fargo saw, his gaze coming to a halt. One bunk was stripped bare of bedding, everything cleaned out from below it, and a neatly tied duffel bag and bedroll had been placed atop the bare mattress. As if waiting to be hurriedly collected, Fargo pondered. He closed the door to the bunkhouse and slid along the outside wall to the back corner. The line of figures, some afoot, some on horseback, had reached the bottom of the shale hills and were headed toward him. Staying in a crouch, he streaked for the trees and reached them only a foot away from where he'd left the Ovaro.

He skidded to a halt, drew a deep breath of relief, and leaned back against a tanbark oak, his eyes on the main house. The pony wagon had been waiting and ready, so he decided to watch and wait. He settled back, a frown wrinkling his brow. It was only a moment until the pony rig came into view from the rear of the house, Ada Carter alone in it. Fargo watched her take the road that circled away from the house before he climbed onto the Ovaro. Staying inside the oaks, he rode along the hillside while he looked down at Ada Carter in the pony rig. She drove well, arms close to her sides, hands held high, a small figure with her thin face all but hidden beneath a flowered bonnet.

Perhaps she had been more nervous than her husband, quick to go along with his lie. If so, she'd be the easiest to reach, Fargo decided. He kept the pony cart in sight, and when the woman turned onto a narrow side road, he spurred the Ovaro forward through the trees and then downward. When the woman rolled around the end of a long curve, she found the big black-and-white horse blocking her path. She reined to a halt and Fargo saw the instant alarm flood her face. He let her wait a moment, fear rising inside her as she stared at him.

"It's not nice to lie. Not healthy, either," he murmured.

"I . . . I don't know what you mean," Ada Carter said. Her lips twitched.

"I think you do, Ada," Fargo said. "I paid a visit to the bunkhouse. I saw Elwood Cord's bunk, all his things cleaned up nice and neat." He saw the panic flood the woman's face as her tongue licked the dryness from her lips. "Why'd your husband send him to kill Willie Magee?" Fargo snapped out.

Ada Carter reeled almost as if she'd been physically struck. "No, no," she said, barely squeezing the words through her lips. "No, he didn't do that. No, never."

"Why'd he lie about Cord working for him, then?" Fargo speared harshly.

Ada swallowed hard, her hands dropping to her lap and tightening into small fists of tension. "He knew Elwood was into something. Simon didn't want to get involved. He wanted his things cleared out," the woman said. "But he didn't send him to kill anybody."

"Maybe," Fargo muttered.

"What are you saying?" Ada Carter frowned.

"Maybe he killed Sam Whitford and Willie Magee knew it, so he had to have Willie killed," Fargo thrust at her.

Ada Carter's eyes closed in horror, her face rigid. "No, no, no," she bit out, finally pulling her eyes open. "Simon didn't kill Sam Whitford, not now, not after all these years of living with it." Her lips drawn back, panic and anguish holding her face, Ada Carter seemed about to burst into tears, but she swallowed hard again and kept her composure in hand.

"Living with what?" Fargo barked.

"Giving Sam Whitford ten percent of the mine's earnings all these years, twenty years now," the woman said. "Twenty years it's been going on."

"Maybe he just got tired of paying up," Fargo said.

"No, not after all the time. Simon accommodated himself to it. It was part of doing business," the woman said.

"Why?" Fargo speared. "Why was he paying ten percent?"

Ada Carter's lips trembled for a moment, but she lifted her head and her thin face took on unexpected strength. "Blackmail, that's why," she snapped out. "A lifetime of blackmail. Yes, Sam Whitford was a blackmailer." She halted, misgivings and fears plainly racing through her mind.

"Give me the rest, all of it," Fargo pressed.

Ada's small figure trembled as she drew a deep breath. "Twenty years ago Simon killed a man. It was over me. Not a fair fight, but Simon did it," Ada Carter said. "Sam Whitford saw it. He agreed to keep silent about it, to say it had been self-defense, for a price." She sighed again and seemed relieved. "There, that's it," she said. "That's why. It's been a shadow all these years, kept away, sometimes almost forgotten. You get used to carrying shadows. They become part of you, part of your life. That's why I know Simon didn't kill Sam Whitford after the party. Why, after all these years? Why all of a sudden? No, never."

Fargo turned the woman's words in his mind. They made a kind of sense, yet there were unexplained holes, Elwood Cord and Willie Magee among them.

"You have to believe me," Ada Carter continued. "What I told you is the truth."

"Maybe all the truth you know," Fargo said, trying to keep the harshness from his voice.

She stared. Her thin face had grown suddenly composed under the flowered bonnet. "It is the truth," she said softly.

"Doesn't suit me enough," Fargo said. "Where were you headed just now?"

"To the quilting bee at Lucy Perkins'," the woman said.

"When you get back, tell your husband I'll be visiting again," Fargo said.

She nodded, then he backed the Ovaro from the road. Ada Carter snapped the reins and drove on, a small woman with more strength than she seemed to have on the surface. She had been shaken, unquestionably afraid, but he wasn't satisfied with her answers. Some of them were true, he was certain, but there were too many other things that did not fit. He let thoughts idle across his mind as he rode, and he reached Bonnie's place as dusk began to slide into dark. He led the horse to the barn.

Bonnie was in the doorway when he returned, the yellow blouse clinging to her firm, high-busted body, her natural pugnaciousness sending out sparks. "What'd you find out?" she demanded, edginess in her voice.

"A few things," he said calmly.

"Such as?"

"Found out I'm hungry," Fargo said.

She stared at him and her eyes softened. "Yes, I expected you might be," she said. "I've a kettle on. Little bit of everything in it." She went into the house, round, firm rear wriggling, and he sat down at the puncheon table. The food she dished out on tin plates was tasty, and she ate along with him. "I'm sorry I flew at you," Bonnie said. "Without even a hello. But all I've done is wonder what you were finding out ever since you left."

He sat back and told her everything Ada Carter had said. She began to simmer and when he finished, she was practically sending out sparks. "Grandpa was no blackmailer," she flung at him. "I don't believe any of it. I don't see why you do."

"She was too upset, too scared for making up stories, especially none that good. I believe some of what she told me," Fargo said.

"Well, I don't believe any of it. Grandpa was no blackmailer. She's lying to save her husband. Simon Carter killed my grandpa for some other reason. She made up all those things she told you," Bonnie insisted. "Elwood Cord worked for him. You know that now. When Simon Carter learned you broke out of jail last night, he had to have Willie Magee killed before you got to him and found out the truth. He sent Cord to make sure Willie didn't tell you anything."

"It reads real well, I'll admit," Fargo said.

"It's as plain as the nose—" she began in exasperation.

"Maybe too plain," Fargo cut in. "We could be headed down the wrong road."

"How?"

"By letting me get in the way," Fargo said. Bonnie frowned in question. "Nobody knew I'd arrive when I did, not even your grandpa. When Hal Comager found me outside the house, somebody realized I'd make the perfect scapegoat. Willie Magee was brought in to make sure of that. I'd doubt he ever knew who killed Sam Whitford. He was dragged in, an afterthought, to make the case against me."

"That doesn't make Simon Carter innocent. Elwood Cord was his man," Bonnie returned.

"You're right, it doesn't. But it doesn't make him guilty, either, not all by itself. Somebody else could have hired Elwood Cord to do in Willie," Fargo said.

"I suppose so." Bonnie frowned. "But why did Ada Carter give you all that fool talk about Grandpa being a blackmailer? Seems she was setting up excuses for her husband killing Grandpa."

"Just the opposite, according to her. She was telling me why he'd no reason to suddenly do it after all these years," Fargo said.

"Lies, all of it," Bonnie snapped angrily, and spun away to stare out of the doorway into the night. He took her by her round shoulders and turned her to face him.

"You want to find the real killer or make another mistake?" he asked, his voice gentler than his words.

She glowered for a moment before answering. "All right, but Simon Carter gets my vote," she said.

"Maybe, but there's too much else that bothers me," Fargo said. "Hal Comager, for one," he added. "He started shooting the minute he saw me outside. There was no reason for him to do that unless he knew Sam Whitford was inside the house dead."

Bonnie's lips fell open in surprise. "You think Hal did it? No, I . . . I can't believe that," she gasped.

63

"For now, I'm just saying he knew," Fargo answered. "What more can you tell me about him?"

Bonnie thought for a moment. "He worked for Grandpa for a long time, but I was never friendly with him. Hal always kept pretty much to himself," she said, thinking back. "He was the loner kind, a very good foreman but never chummy with anybody, not even his men." She paused and Fargo saw the crease deepen on her forehead. "But the past few months he'd become more solitary than usual, sometimes hardly even civil. Didn't bother me any, though. I never had much to do with him, anyway."

Fargo put her answer in a corner of his mind. "Now, let's have the list of who was at that party. Simon and Ada Carter," he began.

"Abe and Mary Floy. He runs the biggest Hereford ranch around here. Egbert Allcomb. He has a contract to ship beef to the army in three states. He uses a lot of Abe Floy's cattle. Harry and Emma Straker. He owns a silver mine near Crazy Peak. And Rob and Betsy Cleaver. His money comes from owning a fleet of riverboats that sail the Missouri and the Mississippi."

"None seems the murdering kind, not on the surface, at least," Fargo said. "But it always surprises me what you find when you start poking around."

"Poke around Simon Carter some more," Bonnie muttered.

When Fargo went to the doorway to gaze into the night, she came to stand beside him. The light behind her silhouetted the contour of one very round, high breast and her pert, upturned nose. Her belligerence was real, he knew, but it was also a shield.

She wore all her emotions on the outside, a quality that made her both vulnerable and dangerously appealing.

"When your grandpa hired me he said he might have to do some manhunting. Got any idea what he might've meant by that?" Fargo asked.

"No." She frowned. "Not in the slightest. It doesn't mean a thing to me."

"He said it. It meant something," Fargo answered firmly.

Bonnie said nothing, but her eyes were fixed into the darkness, her face grown grave.

"What are you thinking?" Fargo asked.

"The funeral's just past noon tomorrow. Such a short time away. I'm going to bed now. I want to be alone with my own thoughts."

"I'll go on my own," he told her, and she paused as she started to turn past him.

"I'm beholden to you, Fargo, no matter how it all ends," she said. "Even if it ends with us fighting." She reached up brushed his cheek with a kiss and hurried off into the adjoining room and closed the door behind her.

He stayed in the doorway for a moment, her light touch lingering. She was not unlike a campfire, he decided, full of crackling sparks yet made of warmth. He pulled the door closed and went into the small extra room, shed clothes, and stretched out on the bed. Bonnie had called Ada Carter's words nothing but lies and excuses, her defensive dismissal made of love and loyalty. But those emotions could be the stuff of blindness, he realized. Everything about this killing was a question mark, and perhaps that included Sam Whitford. He closed his eyes, suddenly tired. There'd be time enough to dig out the truth when he had more than speculation. He slept quickly, the night silent. When he awoke he was rested, his mind and body fresh.

The house was still as he dressed, then paused at Bonnie's closed door. He heard the sounds of rustling petticoats, and he walked outside to the barn. He saddled the Ovaro and rode from the yard, crossed the low hills, and arrived at Sam Whitford's ranch house. He dismounted, pushed the door open, and walked inside the house as silent as the night he'd come upon it. Only there were no lights blazing now and no bludgeoned forms on the study floor.

Fargo moved behind the desk and began to open each drawer, then sat down to examine the papers and letters, deeds and notes he found there. He came upon an IOU for a thousand dollars from Abe Floy and made a mental note of it, though it hardly seemed cause for murder. When he finished going through all he could find in the desk, he wandered around the study and examined the single drawer of a small side table, but found nothing important. He halted in the center of the room. His eyes slowly traveled along the shelves, the books neatly lined in long rows. Papers, notes, personal records, could be lodged inside any one of the books, but he'd need hours of uninterrupted time to check them all. Still, a return visit with Bonnie might be in order, he told himself.

As he walked from the house, the sun was creeping into the noon sky. He rode toward Horsehead, halted a man driving a peddler's wagon, and received directions to Knob Hill. When he saw the low hill with the headstones in a semicircle, a small crowds already gathered by an open gravesite, he circled and came down from the rear of the hill. He halted a half-dozen yards back.

Hal Comager was standing to one side of Bonnie, who was clothed in a black skirt and blouse. A knot of men and women in black attire were clustered together near a row of rigs and surreys, Simon and Ada Carter among them. A slight-built man wearing a preacher's collar and coat held his Bible open, and two burying men waited to one side. Along the other side of the gravesite he saw a line of people he took to be townsfolk paying their respects, one man still wearing his smithy's apron.

The preacher stepped forward. He had a resonant, righteous voice and he lifted his face to the sky as he spoke. "We are here not just to say good-bye. We are here to speed the soul of Sam Whitford to a better place." He halted and lowered his face as a wagon suddenly appeared, moving fast, with Carrie at the reins. Inside the spring wagon were four of Carrie's girls, all in their working clothes, gowns too bright and too tight. Bonnie half-turned and stared at the older woman as the wagon came to a halt and Carrie swung to the ground in her red satin sheath.

Fargo moved the Ovaro down the hillside toward the grave.

"What are you doing here?" he heard Bonnie hiss at Carrie.

"We come to pay our respects," Carrie said.

"Dressed like that? This is a funeral," Bonnie snapped.

"Hell, honey, this is a celebration," Carrie answered. Fargo saw the shock in Bonnie's face as her mouth fell open. "The rest of these fine folks just won't say it out loud," Carrie added.

"You bitch! You dirty-mouthed whore," Bonnie exploded. Her right arm shot out and the slap smashed across Carrie's face with the sharp sound of a derringer going off. Carrie, surprised and stung, staggered backward, and Bonnie leapt forward, arms flailing, fingernails outstretched. Carrie retreated for an instant and then ducked low and swung through Bonnie's flailing, furious attack. Her hard-fisted punch caught Bonnie alongside the jaw, and she immediately went backward and down.

Carrie went after her at once, spitting out curses, bottle blond hair bouncing. She aimed a kick at Bonnie, but the younger girl rolled, bounced to her feet, and head down, barreled into Carrie. Fargo saw the moment of pain flash through Carrie's face as Bonnie's shoulder rammed into her stomach. Wrapping both arms around the taller woman, Bonnie pressed forward and they went down in a tangle of flailing arms and kicking legs, half-sobs and curses from Bonnie, biting fury from Carrie.

Fargo spurred the pinto on and reined up, leaping to the ground as Bonnie yanked Carrie's head around by the hair. "Bitch, rotten, lying bitch," Bonnie spat as she made up for weight and height with pure fury.

"Ow, gaddamn," Carrie yelled. She brought an elbow up that made Bonnie let go of her grip and fall back with a gasp of pain.

The others were looking on transfixed at the sudden explosion of fury. As Bonnie tried to get to her feet, Carrie kicked out, caught her in the side, and sent her sprawling to the edge of the grave. But as

Carrie came at her, aiming another kick, Bonnie twisted away, got a hand around the older woman's ankle and pulled. Carrie went down, flat on her back with a curse and a gasp of pain, and Bonnie was atop her at once, pummeling and clawing as she sobbed in fury. Carrie managed to get her arms up and deflected most of the furious rain of blows, but Bonnie was a raging bundle of fury.

Fargo stepped in, swung one arm around her waist, and yanked her into the air.

"Let me go, you bastard," Bonnie screamed, not looking to see who had her. Her boot raked along his ankle.

"Stop it, damn you," he barked, and shook her as though she were a rag doll. When he stopped, she blinked and focused on him.

"She started it," Bonnie muttered.

"You started it," he snapped as he set her down on her feet.

"She started it by what she said," Bonnie insisted.

"You started it by what you did," Fargo growled. "Now shut up. You said this was a funeral. Act like it." He brushed past her to confront Carrie, who wiped a streak of blood from her forehead.

"Damn little bitch," Carrie muttered, her girls standing behind her.

"You have no cause to come here like this," Fargo said.

"Like hell I don't," the woman snapped. "But I said my piece. I'm not staying." She turned and climbed into the spring wagon, the four girls following. She took the reins, cast a quick glance at him. "You saved her little ass, not mine, you know," she said. "I'd have taken her apart."

"Don't be too sure," Fargo said. "Let's say I saved both your asses."

Carrie gave a grunt, snapped the reins with a flourish, and sent the spring wagon rolling away.

Fargo turned back to the others and saw Bonnie wiping tears and dirt from her face. She marched to the preacher and muttered, and he opened his Bible and began the service again. Bonnie stood stiffly, head bowed, arms tight against her sides.

When it was over, she strode to the roan without looking at him, climbed onto the horse, and rode away. Fargo waited, watched the others begin to move toward their rigs. Simon Carter's quick glance was a mixture of apprehension and an attempt at boldness. Ada didn't look up as she clung to his arm. Hal Comager was the last to turn away, and Fargo stopped him before he reached his horse.

"You knew," Fargo said.

"I knew what?" Comager growled.

"You knew Sam Whitford was dead when you came onto me outside," Fargo said.

"You're crazy, Fargo," the man blustered.

"You knew," Fargo repeated. "The question is, did you know because you did the killing."

"I didn't kill him. You watch your words, mister," Hal said, his hatchet jaw thrusting out still further.

"I'll promise you one thing: I'm going to find out," Fargo said.

The man pulled himself onto his horse. "You stay out of my way, mister," he called, and spurred his horse into a fast canter.

Fargo waited until the man was out of sight before he climbed onto the Ovaro. Comager was the kind to make threats, guilty or not. He had known, and he was damn nervous. The man was fast becoming a larger question mark. But as Fargo rode down the hillside, his thoughts were more on Carrie than Comager. The woman's appearance at the funeral had been an unexpected turn, but it had been her words that stayed with him. They had held a bitterness that was more than sardonic. Perhaps Carrie could supply him with something he still needed: reasons and motives. The only one he had so far was Simon Carter, and that still failed to satisfy.

But first he steered the pinto across the road and over the low hills to Bonnie's ranch, reining to a halt at the door beside the roan. He went into the house and saw her bedroom door shut, but the sound of quiet sobbing was plain. He went into the kitchen, put the pot on the embers, and heated himself a cup of coffee. He made enough noise so she would hear him, but the door stayed closed. He took his coffee outside, sat down on a log, and watched the sun slide toward the distant mountain peaks. He let thoughts idle, but one thing kept pushing at him: there was something hidden about Sam Whitford's killing. The answers, when they came, would not be so simple as blackmail. It was a feeling he had that stayed inside him. He sensed a darkness surrounding the murder, but he still needed more facts, the concrete kind that would let him dig further. As the sun disappeared over the horizon, he went back inside the house.

The door to Bonnie's room remained closed, so he looked into the kettle and found plenty of stew left. He put a fire on under it, realizing he was hungry. There was only silence now from Bonnie's room. He stepped to the closed door. "You'll have

71

plenty of time for hurting and grieving later. Meanwhile, you have to eat and I've got some questions to ask," he called.

"No. Go away," she replied.

He pushed on the door but it moved only slightly. She had a latch on, not a very strong one, he felt. "Come out. I have questions I want answered," he said.

"Go away." Her voice was muffled and truculent.

"You wanted my help," he reminded her.

"Not anymore, not after you standing up for that whore at the funeral," Bonnie muttered. "You can go away."

"I didn't stand up for her."

"You said I started it. That's standing up for her," Bonnie returned.

"That's truth," Fargo said. "Now, get your little ass out here."

There was a long moment of silence. "Go away." Now there was as much hurt as anger in her tone.

"Dammit, girl, I've had enough of this," Fargo said. He stepped back, raised his leg, and kicked out with all the strength of his powerful thigh muscles. The door flew open in a spray of splinters. Bonnie looked up in surprise. She sat cross-legged atop a wide brass bed, but she swung to the floor with a flash of pretty, round knees. "No damn-fool attitudes," Fargo roared from the doorway. "I've neither the mind nor the time for that."

"I'm not letting anyone like her talk about Grandpa like that," Bonnie muttered.

"You can be righteous on your own time, when it's over," Fargo shot back. "Right now I want you thinking, not grousing." She scowled back but kept her pretty lips tightly closed. "You know if Simon

72

Carter paid regular visits to your grandpa—say, once a month?" he asked.

"Sure, he visited regularly. All of Gramps' friends did. That doesn't prove anything," Bonnie snapped.

"Not by itself. It's part of making a pattern, putting together a lot of little things. Sometimes they fit, sometimes they don't," Fargo said. "I'll be gone for the rest of the night. I want you to spend your time thinking about where your grandpa might've kept his personal papers. Man like him has to have had them someplace. I took a look around the study and came up with nothing."

"I told you, he never brought me into his other world," she said.

"Maybe not on purpose, but you were close. Somewhere, over the years, you had to have seen something, heard something. Maybe you put it out of your mind. Well, now I want you to bring it back. Think about it, think back hard, think on it awake and dream on it asleep. I'll see you come morning."

"Where are you going?" she asked.

He hesitated, thought about telling her, and decided against it. "Snooping around on my own," he said. "Maybe pay Simon Carter a visit."

She accepted the answer and her scowl faded as he left the house and swung onto the pinto.

He rode into the night, crossed a hill, and took the road that led into Horsehead. He rode slowly, knowing Carrie would be there. All he had to do was to get her to explain her remark at the funeral. It shouldn't be hard to do, he realized, yet you never could be sure with any woman. Bonnie's kind could explode into refusal. Carrie's type could retreat into obstinacy. But he had to try. He had to find out if explanations offered answers.

4

Carrie's Bunkhouse was crowded when Fargo entered, the bar full and most of the tables taken. The girls moved casually among the customers, some already ensconced at tables and on jean-clad laps. He spotted Carrie's red satin figure near the corner of the bar. She gave a wry smile when she saw him approaching, and he was again struck by her good looks, despite the excess of makeup.

"I expected you'd be back," the woman said when he halted before her full-busted figure.

"Want some explanations," he said.

"No explanations. I said my piece," Carrie answered. "Who are you, anyway?"

"Name's Fargo . . . Skye Fargo."

"Why do you want explanations?"

"I'm going to find Sam Whitford's killer."

The woman's dark-blue eyes clouded. "You do that," she said.

"I still want explanations," Fargo said.

She didn't answer, but even if she had, he couldn't have heard it as a shot exploded with a roar inside the room. He dropped, an instinctive reaction, his hand yanking the Colt from its holster as he hit the floor. He turned his head and saw three men come into the dance hall, two just inside the door, the third striding across the center of the room. All held heavy Hawken buffalo rifles, and the one in the center held his pointed directly at Carrie.

"Anybody moves gets blasted," the man roared. From his almost prone position on the floor, Fargo took in a tall figure with heavy, long black hair falling from beneath a shapeless black hat, a long, hollow-cheeked face with wild, staring eyes. The man stopped in front of Carrie, perhaps a half-dozen feet from the woman. "I told you I'd be back, bitch," he snarled.

Fargo's glance went to Carrie. Though she swallowed hard, she showed no sign of fear. "And I'm saying the same thing. Get the hell out of my place," Carrie threw back at him.

"I'm taking the girl this time. Where is she?" the man roared.

"She's not here," Carrie said, and refused to flinch under the wild stare.

"Don't shit me," the man roared. "Get her out here."

"She's not here," Carrie repeated firmly.

The man raised the rifle an inch. Fargo swore silently. If he could turn fast enough to bring the Colt around and get a shot off at the wild-eyed figure, the two nearest the door would surely fill him with lead. "Call her or I'll blast a hole right through you, bitch," the man said. His eyes flicked across the room. Everyone stayed frozen, he saw, afraid and uncertain, unwilling to risk their own necks and unsure they could save Carrie's. "The last time, bitch," the man said, his voice rising in wildness. But Carrie met the man's staring, wild eyes with dark contempt, Fargo saw. Damn, he thought, throwing another glance at the two near the door. They were the ones he had to take down first. He slid his arm along the floor, and brought the Colt closer to his face as, with his other hand, he started to press down against the boards.

"Here I am," the girl's voice called out.

Fargo stopped and looked at the small, dark-haired girl in a green gown pushing her way from behind the onlookers. He felt a stab of surprise and admiration go through him. Carrie had shown she held an unexpected strength of character inside her, and now he was seeing an unexpected kind of loyalty. The girl came into the center of the floor, and the wild-eyed man half-turned to her.

"Well, now, that's better," he gloated. But he had turned his back and Fargo seized the instant. He whipped around, brought the Colt up, and fired, the first shot catching the nearest man by the door full in the chest. Before he slammed into the wall, Fargo's second shot hurtled into the other's midsection and the man collapsed as the rifle fell from his hands. But the wild-eyed figure had whirled, as Fargo knew he would, firing as he did.

Fargo didn't try to roll away. Instead, he flung himself forward and felt the rifle shots graze his back as he slammed into the man's ankles. With a curse, the man toppled forward, unable to keep his balance. Fargo brought one knee up, caught the

77

man's inner thigh, and sent him sprawling sideways. The man, on one knee, tried to bring the rifle around to shoot again, but Fargo fired a bullet that caught the man under the chin. The top of his head seemed to come off with his hat as he arched backward and hit the floor with a heavy, crunching sound. A stream of red flowed from the top of his head, quickly turning the thick black hair a sodden rust color.

"Jesus," Fargo heard Carrie breathe as he pushed to his feet. "That was some fancy shooting."

"Sometimes there's no time to miss," he said, and holstered the Colt. He stared down at the man for a moment, his eyes questioning when they returned to Carrie.

"I threw him out a few nights ago. He was a crazy then, too, insisted on taking Pam with him. I didn't believe him when he said he'd be coming back for her. I thought it was just more crazy talk," the woman said.

"Your mistake," Fargo commented.

She nodded and drew a deep breath that stretched the bustline of the satin gown to its limits. She gestured to two men with mops. "Clean the place up. Take them all outside and call Seth Owen," she ordered. As the men moved to obey, Carrie called across the room and flashed a wide and reassuring smile. "It's over. Everybody gets a drink on the house." The crowd took up a murmur of approval as they settled down. She turned to Fargo, her dark-blue eyes narrowed as she studied his chiseled handsomeness. "Seems I owe you, Fargo, more than I've ever owed anybody, my life," she said.

"You can do some explaining," he said.

"Maybe something more," she said.

"We'll see." He shrugged and a smile touched his lips.

"First room at the top of the stairs. Go in and wait. I'll be along soon as I can," she said.

"Sounds fine." He nodded and made his way to the stairs at the back of the dance hall. He brushed through a curtain and went up to a dimly lighted corridor with rooms branching out from both sides. He halted at the first room, the door painted a bright pink, turned the knob, and stepped inside. He found himself in a fair-sized room decorated in pink drapes and yellow and pink ruffles on almost everything, including the corner posts of the big bed. A dresser covered with powder and perfume flasks took up one wall, and a small lamp covered with a pink shade gave the room a dusty-rose light. He sat down on the edge of the bed, stretched his long legs, and closed his eyes while he waited.

He dozed at least twice before the door finally opened and he sat up as Carrie entered. She halted before him, her smile almost weary though it warmed her pleasant face. "You're not the ordinary dance-hall madam," he told her. "You showed me that much. Your girls know it, too. They showed me that."

"You're not the ordinary trail rider. You showed me that," she said.

"I won't be turned aside by sweet words and soft lips, if that's what you mean," Fargo said.

Her smile was wry. "Why don't we try?" She raised one hand and unhooked the clasp at the back of her dress. The bodice fell limply, exposing deep, heavy breasts, rounded softly at the bottom of each cup, brownish-pink nipples encircled with brownish-pink areolae. She slid her hands down and pushed the rest of the red satin sheath away and stood naked before him. She had round, wide hips and a slight curve to her belly that ended in a deep, curly mat. Her legs were as firm and youthful as the rest of her body, and she enjoyed the appreciation she saw in his eyes. "My girls usually take care of this kind of thing. It's been a long time since I've tended to someone," she whispered.

"What are you telling me?" Fargo asked as he quickly shed his clothes.

"I'm telling you that this is real special."

"Oh. I thought you were telling me you were out of practice," he commented.

Her eyes flared. "Bastard," she murmured as he pulled off the last of his clothes. She pressed against him, pushing him back onto the soft bed. Her skin was warm against his, soft and pliant, and her lips found his with a hungry, open kiss. As her full breasts flattened into his chest, the brown-pink tips stiffened. She raised herself over him and brought one breast to his lips. He drew in the firm nipple, then sucked in a mouthful of the soft flesh. Carrie gasped in delight. "God, oh God, yes . . . yes, good, so good," she murmured as she rubbed her breast back and forth against the warm wetness of his lips.

He lifted his thighs and pressed down on the bed as he rolled over with her, still sucking hungrily on her breast. She screamed and clutched tightly at his hair. He pulled away, took the other soft mound, and drew it deep into his mouth while Carrie moaned and twisted beneath him. Her hands moved up and down the sides of his body, pressed into his hips, his legs, his thighs. His own groan of pleasure blended with hers as she closed one hand firmly around him. "Oh, oh, yes," she breathed as she stroked his hot, thick strength. Her legs opened, lifted, her thighs against him as she slid her belly back and forth, up and down against his pelvis.

"Uuuuuh . . . uuuuh," she gasped, clinging to him, arms encircling his neck, burying his mouth in her heaving breasts. He slid one hand down her body, a firm pressure as he moved over her abdomen, across her smooth belly, and into the thick, curly patch. "Yes, yes," Carrie urged, her hips twisting, turning, reaching up to him. His hand gently ran farther down, pushed between her legs to the moistness of her thighs. He rubbed his fingers slowly along her skin. "My God, oh, my God," Carrie groaned with unrestrained surprise and passion. Her fingers curled, found him again, and pulled.

"Take me, dammit . . . oh, Jesus, take me." Her cries were almost savage now, and her hips heaved upward, more in demand than entreaty. He raised himself over her. She guided his enormous length with a warm hand and groaned with pleasure as he slid deep into her, held a moment, slid farther. "Aaaaah . . . aaaah, oh, God, yes, oh, yes," she murmured. She began to work with him at once, pumping her torso up and down, creating her own erotic sensation. He felt himself responding, pulsing, gathering. But she slowed, pushed gently, then quickened her motions with a wild guttural groan. Again, as he felt himself start to spiral, she slowed, letting ecstasy toy with ecstasy, prolonging each delirious moment. Suddenly, with a tremendous groaning cry, she threw her head back and rolled it from side to side. Her legs tightened around him in the climax of climaxes. Their ecstasy exploded beyond the senses, and his own groan of pleasure again joined her cry as spasms pulsed through his loins.

She stayed pressed against him, her breath a heavy, gasping sound in his ear until slowly she relaxed her muscles, her thighs pulling away from him, her arms dropping from his neck. She lay still on the bed, drawing in deep breaths. Little lines of time stretched down her throat and spread from the corners of her eyes, he saw, but she remained a surprisingly attractive and youthful woman. She smiled as his eyes moved over her.

"Reading?" she asked. "The world leaves its marks."

"On everybody," he said.

She rose up on her elbows, her breasts sliding to the sides. "Was I too out of practice?" she asked with a touch of acid.

He grinned back. "One for you," he said.

"You're an exciting man, Fargo," she said. "I'm glad I owed you."

"You figure you're paid up?" he asked.

"Much as I can," she answered.

"Try again," he said. "I still want that explanation."

She remained silent, wrestling with thoughts. When she sat up straight, her breasts swayed in unison. "You wouldn't settle for another go-round?" she asked, sliding a sidelong glance at him.

"Sure," he said. "After the explanation."

The woman frowned, her lips pursed as she peered at him. "Is it really that important to you? Or is it the girl?" she asked.

"The man hired me, he was killed, and I was accused of it. It's important," Fargo said. He put his hand out and cupped one full breast, his thumb gliding slowly across the firm tip. "Afterward," he said, and she lowered her eyes as he drew his hand back. "You called the funeral a celebration. Why?" he asked.

"Because most everybody there wanted him dead," she said. "They didn't come to mourn, they came to enjoy."

"Spell it out for me, Carrie," Fargo said, and leaned on one elbow.

She drew her legs up, turned, and lay half on her stomach, still looking like a woman half her age. "The girl thinks her grandfather was a saint. She idolizes him. Why not? He always gave her whatever she wanted. She was his pride and joy and he was wonderful to her, warm and understanding. But she was the only one. Sam Whitford was a real bastard," the woman said. "He cheated, blackmailed, pressured, bullied, and forced people to do what he wanted. But he always kept that side of himself from her. He kept it from a lot of people. But not the ones who really knew him."

"You saying anybody at the funeral might have killed him?" Fargo questioned.

"Guess I am," Carrie agreed.

"I know about Simon Carter. He claims he was being blackmailed all these years by Sam Whitford," Fargo told her.

"He was," the woman said. "So was Harry Straker. He's been forking over one half of what the mine earns every year to Sam Whitford."

"Why?" Fargo asked.

"Twenty years ago Harry Straker had a partner in the mining operation. The partner was killed one day in an accident in one of the mine shafts. The way I put it together is that Sam Whitford knew it was no accident. His price was half of whatever the mine earns."

Fargo frowned at Carrie. "Abe Floy have a reason, too?" he asked.

"I heard that Sam Whitford tricked Abe Floy out of his ranch," Carrie said. "He let Floy buy a big herd by telling him he'd be there with the cash. But he wasn't. Floy lost the herd and everything he had. Then Sam Whitford showed up with the cash, bought everything dirt-cheap, and brought Abe Floy back in to be the front man. Abe Floy, a broken man, took the offer, but you can be sure he never forgot what had been done to him."

"Where'd you find out all this?" Fargo asked.

"You know that everything comes out in a saloon and with a warm girl sooner or later. You listen to little bits and pieces and soon you learn all of it," the woman said.

Fargo nodded, well aware of the truth in her answer. "Egbert Allcomb have his reasons to kill Sam Whitford?" he asked. "Seeing as how he and Abe Floy traded together."

"I don't know, but I'd guess he most likely did," Carrie answered.

"Anybody else you know about?" Fargo pressed.

"Hal Comager," Carrie said. Fargo's interest spiraled. "He's worked for poor man's wages for all these years because Sam Whitford told him he'd get the ranch one day. The girl had her own place. She'd no need for it and Sam had promised it to

Hal. But six months ago, Hal found out that Whitford had agreed to sell it to a buyer from the East— Pennsylvania, I think." She paused in thought for a moment. "You could say that with Whitford dead and the ranch still unsold, Hal would have a good chance to get it," she added.

Fargo let her words hang in his mind: betrayal, revenge, desperation—all of them reason enough for murder. And Hal Comager had known Sam Whitford was dead when he came riding up shooting and accusing. Comager was rapidly moving to first place, Fargo decided. He turned his attention back to Carrie, who stretched sensually out on the bed. "I take it that Rob Cleaver is not involved with any of this, seeing as how his money comes from riverboats," Fargo said.

"Don't be sure. I know that Sam Whitford invested in those riverboats, but I don't know anything else," Carrie said.

Fargo drew a long sigh and decided not to mark Cleaver off entirely.

Carrie turned, slid to him, and brought her breasts up against his abdomen, pressing down and reveling in the pressure of skin against skin. He took her by the hair, lifted her face gently, and her mouth parted for him. "No more talk," she breathed.

"No more talk," he echoed, and curled his hand around her full breasts. She gave a tiny shudder of pleasure and rose over him. In the dusty-rose light he made love to her again, and she responded with all her body and experience. When she lay exhausted beside him and he felt his own wonderful tiredness, she closed her eyes and slept.

He stayed until the night had turned to dawn

"What'd you learn about your business?" she asked, the sharpness still in her voice.

He paused and looked at her calmly. "I learned your grandpa was a real bastard." He was ready. Her arm tightened and he ducked as the coffee mug flew over his head.

"You get out of here," Bonnie shouted, and started at him, fire in her brown eyes. He seized her wrist as she aimed a blow at him, whirled her around, and sent her crashing into the wall. She bounced off, blinked and stood still.

"Now you're going to listen to me," he said. "Until I'm finished. Then you can talk."

She scowled at him, but she stayed in place as he told her everything he'd heard. The scowl turned into a dark, frowning glower when he finished, and she waited a long moment before saying anything. "Where'd you hear all this?" she asked.

"Carrie told me," he answered, expecting the snort she gave out.

"And you believe it?" she spat.

"I'm going to follow it up for myself," he said. "But I can't see any reason for her to make it up."

"To blacken a good man's name. That's all her kind needs," Bonnie threw back.

"What if she's right?" Fargo asked.

"No, she can't be, not about Grandpa or any of the others," Bonnie insisted.

"That include Hal Comager? You said yourself he'd been keeping more to himself than usual the past few months," Fargo reminded her.

"That doesn't make him a murderer or Grandpa a terrible person," Bonnie countered. "I don't believe any of it. She was making up stories."

"Why?" Fargo speared.

"I don't know why," Bonnie answered hotly. "Maybe to impress you. Maybe she just likes lying about people."

"And Ada Carter's story was made up too?" he pressed.

"Yes," Bonnie retorted.

Fargo fell silent. She would not accept anything else now, not until it became impossible to believe anything else. He would wait until he had more than Carrie's words to convince her.

"I asked you to think about something," he said. "You come up with any answers?"

"No," she said, but he caught the instant of hesitation in her voice.

"Don't play games with me, Bonnie," he warned.

"I'm not playing games," she snapped. "I haven't remembered anything yet."

"Keep thinking. He had to keep personal records someplace. Maybe we ought to just go to the ranch and start taking it apart until we find them," Fargo thought aloud.

"Tomorrow," Bonnie said quickly. "I have shearing and clipping to do the rest of today. I'll go with you tomorrow."

"All right," he agreed. "You do your chores. I want to do some riding."

"What kind of riding?" she questioned.

"Checking-around riding. I'll see you tonight." She nodded, unsmiling, waiting by the house while he rode away.

He crossed the nearest hillside and went down a road where he spied a man driving a pony cart. It was the preacher. "Making your rounds, Preacher?" he asked pleasantly.

"I am. You're Bonnie's friend, the one that was at the funeral," the preacher said. "Terrible tragedy, that."

"Seems so," Fargo agreed. "You know Sam Whitford well, Preacher?"

"No, he was never a churchly man, unfortunately, though he saw to it that Bonnie was brought up properly."

"Can you tell me where Abe Floy's place is? The Strakers', too?" Fargo asked. "And also Egbert Allcomb's and the Cleaver ranch. Want to pay my respects to Sam Whitford's friends."

"Go north along the road. You'll reach Allcomb's first. The others are spread out from there in a loose half-circle, some a few miles farther west," the minister said.

"Much obliged, Preacher." Fargo nodded and turned the Ovaro north. When he reached the first large house, he turned aside, positioned the Ovaro for a moment, then put the horse into a gallop until he reached Sam Whitford's ranch. He halted, cast a glance up at the sun, and turned the horse around. He rode hard again, this time to Abe Floy's place, and halted at a clump of trees nearby to take the position of the sun again.

The day had come to an end when he finished the last trip, and he halted in the darkness, dismounted, and let the horse drink from a shallow stream. But he'd found out what he'd wanted to know: any one of them could have left the party and returned to kill Sam Whitford within an hour after the party ended. None could be eliminated because of distance or time. He began the trip back to Bonnie's under a half-moon sky.

He rode slowly, moved down the last low hill and onto the road bordered by black oak on both sides. He sat relaxed in the saddle when three white-tailed deer suddenly bolted away twenty yards to his right. He slowed and saw a fourth, tail thrust upward in alarm, leap to the left of the road. His eyes grew narrow. He hadn't frightened them. He was too far away. Something else, closer to them, had set them off. The road stretched ahead, a long curve, the route anyone would take to Bonnie's ranch. The way he'd be expected to take, Fargo thought, slowing the horse again. He let the Ovaro walk down the center of the road toward the spot where the deer had bounded away, tensing his muscles and straining his ears. But the border of trees and brush were silent. His lips pulled back in a grimace. Something had made the deer bolt and he wouldn't take chances.

At the place where the deer had taken flight, he dug his heels hard into the horse's side and dropped flat across the black neck. The pinto bolted into a gallop as Fargo pressed himself against the side of the powerful neck. Shots exploded—two from the trees at the right, another set from the left. He felt the bullets pass only a fraction of an inch away from him as the pinto raced on. His ambushers continued to fire, but he was past the direct cross fire. He opened his hands, let the reins drop, and toppled from the saddle as the horse raced on.

He hit the ground, Colt in hand, landed on one shoulder, and rolled to his side, positioned himself, and lay still. Two figures burst from the trees, one from each side. "We got him," one yelled as they ran forward. Fargo lay motionless and saw the third figure come from the trees, a few yards beyond the others. He let the first two run closer before he lifted the Colt and fired two shots at almost point-blank range. Their jaws dropped as they spotted the raised Colt. They tried to twist aside, but it was too late. His shots hurtled into both figures almost simultaneously and the two men shook, staggered, fell into each other, and collapsed onto the ground together. Fargo flung himself into a roll toward the brush to his right as the third man fired two shots. The Trailsman whirled, raised the Colt to fire, and glimpsed the hatchet-jawed face in the moonlight as the man dropped to one knee. He pulled the gun down and fired low. He wanted Hal Comager alive. His shot grazed Comager's left leg, and the man went down, firing three shots that whistled close by.

Comager dived into tree cover and Fargo paused, his jaw tight. The man had fired five shots. Fargo half-rose, started out of the brush, and leapt backwards instantly. But he got what he wanted as Comager fired again, the sixth shot, from inside the tree cover. This time Fargo leapt from the brush and stayed in the open as he raced for the trees where Comager had fired. He saw the man come into the open, the gun still in hand, and halted in surprise as Comager barreled toward him with a roar of desperate fury. Fargo braced himself, dropped the Colt into its holster, and let Comager's bull-like charge almost reach him. The man raised his six-gun to bring it down in a clublike blow, and Fargo bent his knees as he brought up a short left hook that landed flush on the charging man's jaw and sent a shock through his arm and shoulder. But Hal Comager halted as though he'd struck a wall, his head snapping back. Fargo's right cross landed at exactly the same spot, spinning Hal in a complete circle before he hit the ground.

Fargo stepped to the man, used his foot to turn him on his back, and waited for Comager to finally regain consciousness. When the man blinked, tried to lift his head, and fell back onto the ground again, Fargo took a step backward, reloaded his Colt while he waited again. Comager groaned and shook his head as he struggled to a sitting position. He stared up at the big man waiting in front of him, his hatchet jaw still hanging loosely. "You want to tell me about killing Sam Whitford?" Fargo asked.

Comager shook his head and winced with pain. "Didn't kill him," he muttered.

"You just as much as said so," Fargo growled.

"No, didn't kill him," Comager muttered again.

"Bullshit. That's why you tried to kill me just now. You were afraid I'd pin it on you," Fargo said.

Comager looked up at him, a dull anger in his eyes. "That's right. That's what I was afraid of," he said. "I didn't do it, but I figured you'd find out I had a reason and stick me with it." He paused, swallowed hard, and tried to look defiant. "Yes, I found him before you did and I ran for the same reason. I didn't want anyone thinking I did it. I rounded up some of the men in town and said I'd seen somebody hanging around the ranch earlier."

"And there I was, convenient as all hell," Fargo said.

Comager nodded and pushed himself to his feet. "But I didn't kill Sam Whitford," he muttered.

"You had reason," Fargo said. "You want to tell me about it?"

The man's eyes grew wary. "I didn't say I did. I said you'd find something and maybe make it stick."

"I know about his plan to sell the ranch instead of leaving it to you," Fargo said.

Comager's eyes widened. "Carrie," the man shot out. "She's the only one that knew about that beside me. Goddamn her."

"She said you weren't the only one with a reason," Fargo continued.

Comager's eyes narrowed. "She talks too goddamn much," he growled. "But I bet she didn't tell you anything about *her* reasons, did she?"

Fargo frowned. "Her reasons?" he echoed.

"Shit, she had as much reason to kill Sam Whitford as anybody," Comager said. "He was her silent partner. He took half of everything the place made, and she hated his guts for it."

"How do you know that?" Fargo questioned.

"I saw her paying him off once and she told me then. It was a secret deal for years. Ask her yourself," Comager said belligerently.

"I might just do that," Fargo said.

"You want to shoot me for dry-gulching you, go ahead," Comager thrust at him. "But I didn't kill Sam Whitford and you can't prove I did."

"Not yet," Fargo said, but the words hung in his mind. Comager was right in that he had no proof of his killing Sam Whitford. While he didn't accept the man's denial, he couldn't reject it completely, not with all the unanswered questions still hanging in midair. And now another had been added, Fargo grunted inwardly. "I ought to put a hole in you," he said. "I will next time. You can count on it." He stepped back and holstered the Colt. "Get your horse and get out of here before I change my mind."

Hal stepped backward, limping on the leg where the bullet had grazed him. A thin trickle of red stained his Levi's. He turned and hurried into the trees.

Fargo waited until the man emerged on his horse and disappeared into the night. There was no gratitude in Hal Comager, he was certain. His kind thought they were owed a second chance, particularly if he were actually innocent. The man was still a danger. Fargo turned and gave a low whistle; the Ovaro appeared from down the road.

Fargo climbed onto the horse, but he didn't go on toward Bonnie's place. Instead, he turned toward Horsehead, his mouth a thin line. He rode with slow deliberation until he reached town. Carrie's Bunkhouse was in full swing.

Carrie saw him the moment he entered and met him as he pushed through the crowd. He took her by the elbow and guided her toward the stairs at the rear of the house. "What are you doing, Fargo?" Carrie frowned, trying to pull her arm free. But his grip was firm. He pushed her to the top of the stairs.

"This'll just take a minute." He kept his hold until he reached her room and pulled her inside. "You've got to be more careful." Carrie frowned. "About your memory. It seems to be slipping. You left somebody important off that list you gave me." A veil dropped over her eyes. "I can see why," he added.

She turned aside, her lips pursed. "I didn't want to be included with the others," she said. "I didn't do it and I didn't want you to think maybe I had." She lifted her eyes to his and searched the cold stare he had fastened upon her. "That's what you're thinking now, isn't it?"

"You get the cigar," Fargo said. "Maybe I wouldn't be if you'd leveled with me." She made no reply, so he brought her face up to his. "You want to give it a try now?" he asked.

She shrugged, made a helpless little motion with her hands. "A woman named Ellie Hodd had the place before me. When I bought it from her, she left without telling me I'd bought Sam Whitford, too," she said. "I tried to get rid of him, but he wouldn't hear of it. Fact was he told me he'd have me closed up by the sheriff if I didn't keep up the arrangement he had with Ellie Hodd. I had no choice but to go along."

"And wait for a way out," Fargo added.

"I hated him, I'll admit that. He was draining me, taking half the money and paying none of the expenses," the woman said. "But I didn't kill him."

"Seems that's the most popular line in these parts," Fargo said.

"You ever hear of believing someone?" Carrie asked.

"I'm slow at believing," Fargo said.

She stepped to him, pressed her mouth to his, her tongue darting out and pulling back at once. But the touch was memory and promise. "Maybe that will help you," she said, and walked from the room.

He followed her downstairs, left her at the corner of the bar, and walked from the dance hall without looking back. He climbed onto the pinto and rode from town, a sour taste in his mouth. Her excuse for lying to him had been no better than Hal Comager's. But he hadn't rejected Comager's entirely and he couldn't do less with Carrie. But he damn sure couldn't accept the excuse either.

When he reached Bonnie's place, the moon was near the midnight sky. He was surprised to see Bonnie still up, clad in a floor-length pink nightdress, a pink bow in the center of a round neckline.

"More pleasure?" she slid at him.

"Not exactly, unless you call being shot at and lied to pleasure," Fargo said, and sat down to tell her what the evening had brought. Her eyes had grown round when he finished.

"They're both lying," she said. "Grandpa wouldn't do the things they're accusing him of doing. They're just trying to give themselves excuses."

"There's not much excuse for cold-blooded murder," Fargo commented.

"A judge can be sympathetic. A jury can take reasons into account," Bonnie muttered. "But they're all lying about Grandpa."

"Maybe tomorrow will answer that," Fargo said. "We'll go over the house inch by inch. A man like Sam Whitford must have kept personal records someplace. We need to find them. They ought to tell us something."

"Good night," Bonnie said abruptly. She turned and stomped into the adjoining room, slamming the door behind her—small, pugnacious figure lost inside the long nightdress.

Fargo was pulling off his clothes before he reached the bed in the next room and stretched across the mattress. The day had held a few surprises. As he lay awake, unable to quickly fall asleep despite his fatigue, he wondered why he continued to have trouble accepting Hal Comager or Carrie as Sam

Whitford's killer. If their reasons weren't lies, they were more than enough. Men had been killed for far less than greed, blackmail, and broken promises. But something still bothered him, something that nagged just beneath the surface logic of the mind. But he needed more than he had to turn shadows into shapes, so he pushed aside further speculation and let sleep drift over him.

But he slept poorly, tossing and battling wakefulness. Dimly, he fought the uneasiness and managed to sleep until the moon slid low across the deep night sky. He woke and sat up. Something was wrong, he grimaced as he swung from the bed and pulled on trousers. That inner sense jabbed at him, the instinct he had learned never to ignore. He strapped on his gun belt as he left the room and went to the front door, opened it enough to see out, and peered into the night, his ears tuned to pick up every little sound. But he saw nothing and heard only the usual night sounds—the croak of a bullfrog, the hum of insect noises, the rustle of trees in the night breeze.

He closed the door and stepped into the main room. He cast a quick glance at Bonnie's door, saw it was closed, and was turning away when his eyes jerked back to the door. It wasn't closed, he frowned, the edge of the door leaning against the frame. It had been pulled there to look closed without risking the sound of the door latch snapping shut. In one long stride he was through the door, staring at the empty bed in the center of the room.

"Damn," he bit out, grabbing his shirt and throwing it on as he raced from the house. He crossed to the barn and saw the roan was gone. He swore again as he saddled the Ovaro. In minutes he was racing across the front yard and into the hills. He didn't need to find her tracks. He knew exactly where she'd gone. The only question was how much of a head start she had.

He sent the pinto at a gallop across the first hill, down the other side, and along the bottom flatland until he took the shorter way across the last hill. When he crested the rise and cut through the stand of black oak, he frowned. A soft orange glow suddenly colored the darkness ahead of him, flickering, glowing brighter. Fargo cursed as he sent the Ovaro full out. The orange glow continued to grow brighter and suddenly burst into form as he reached the house. Flames shot from the rooftop in the center, and smoke and flickering firelight danced along the window ledges of both wings. A sudden whoosh of air sent a huge tongue of flame bursting through one window, and Fargo leapt from the horse and started toward the door. He halted as the staccato sound of hoofbeats cut through the hiss of the flames. He glimpsed the horse galloping away from the rear of the building, a lone rider flattened low in the saddle. He halted and wondered for an instant if, in some misguided sense of protectiveness, Bonnie had set the blaze and now fled. Protectiveness had sent her sneaking into the night to reach the house alone, and he wondered if he should pursue the fleeing rider. But he cursed as, off to the right near the end of the blazing house, he spotted the roan. She was trapped in the inferno.

Ducking low, he raced through the door and met a blast of scorching air. He ducked away, dropped to one knee, and tied his kerchief around his face.

Gray-blue smoke rolled across the room, but another bursting window drew it spiraling upward. She was not in the living room. Tongues of flame licked the furniture and covered the walls as he dropped to his hands and knees. Another billow of gray-blue smoke rolled at him. Crawling forward, he stayed under the smoke as it swept over him, like a rug being unrolled. He made his way along the hall, flinched back from the inferno that blazed in the kitchen, and reached the study. Somehow the fire had not yet caught hold.

But the room was heavy with smoke, so he stayed low and peered along the floor, his face pressed to the boards. No small, crumpled shape lay in the room, so he crawled out. The heat was becoming almost more than he could stand. He fought his way down the hallway and heard the crackling sound of flame leaping across the air from wall to wall. The terrible hiss of a new burst of fire resounded from all parts of the house, and he peered back to a solid wall of fire consuming the west section of the house.

He tried to rise and was instantly engulfed in choking, acrid smoke. He dropped to the floor again. Crawling on his belly as the smoke pressed lower, he came to another door, which he pushed open. It was the master bedroom, yet untouched by flame, but wisps of smoke danced along the ceiling where the roof above was burning furiously. He guessed it would only take minutes before the ceiling collapsed. It was a large room, two dressers and a heavy wood double bed near the far end. Smoke was pouring in from the hall through the open door. Fargo crawled forward as he saw the leg poking out from behind the far side of the bed. He rose, ignoring the smoke, and ran. Bonnie lay between the bed and the wall, a small red gash across her forehead.

Smoke was quickly growing heavy inside the room, so he dropped to his hands and knees and began to pull her along the floor. He had just reached the doorway when a blast of searing air shot past and a ball of fire came rolling down the hallway. He rose, lifted Bonnie in a fireman's carry, and began to run down the corridor. He heard a sharp cracking sound and flung himself sideways as a piece of the roof crashed down to shower him with sparks. He felt the house shudder and glanced back to see the entire west section collapse. He knew that the rest of the house would come crashing down in a matter of minutes, but he was forced to halt when a piece of the outside wall fell in a burst of flames across the floor. But the night air lay just beyond it, perhaps the only way out. Another piece of the roof collapsed with a roar and a hiss and another shower of flame.

Fargo took a deep breath, drew a firmer hold on Bonnie, and charged forward. He ran across the fallen section of wall and felt the waves of heat come up at him. The flames licked at his legs, and he winced with pain at the fiery touch.

But he kept running, kept driving himself across the molten-hot carpet of wooden cinders and burning planking. He gratefully gasped in deep drafts of the cool night air as he stumbled into the open. He felt the earth under his feet, and swinging Bonnie to the ground, he flung himself down and rolled back and forth across the ground until the flames that had caught at his clothes were snuffed out. He pushed to his hands and knees and made his way to where Bonnie lay. Taking her by both wrists, he dragged her away from the billowing clouds of gray smoke that rose from the furiously burning house. He stopped when he was far from the acrid smoke, and he sat down beside her, still gulping in deep breaths. The ranch house burned.

Bonnie moaned and he quickly shifted his eyes to her. She stirred, half-turned, looked around, and suddenly sat bolt upright, staring at the house.

"Oh, my God. Oh, good God," she breathed.

"You're damn lucky, girl," Fargo growled. She turned, her brown eyes wide. "I figure you'd be about roasted by now."

"You pulled me out," she said.

"I did. But I thought about it for a minute."

Bonnie's eyes dropped downward and he saw contrition fight through the normal pugnaciousness of her face. "I guess I deserved that," she murmured.

"No arguing that," Fargo agreed. "What happened in there?"

"I was hit. I never saw who did it. I don't know how many there were."

"One," Fargo snorted grimly, and fell silent, his eyes on the house. It was still burning, but now there was more smoke than flame.

"Aren't you going to ask me why I came here?" she queried with a touch of surprise in her voice.

"Don't have to," Fargo said. "I know why." She held her eyes on him, allowing curiosity but nothing more. "You were afraid, honey," he told her. "Behind all the sound and fury you were afraid maybe it wasn't all lies about your grandpa." She conceded nothing in her gaze but he saw her lips grow tight. "You remembered a place where he may have kept his personal records and decided to have a look at them yourself first."

She pulled her eyes away and stared at the burning house, smoking ashes and a few heavy timbers still standing, blackened and charred. "There was a wall safe near his bed. I came to open it," she said, her voice hardly above a whisper.

"Somebody else had the same idea," Fargo added.

"I don't know." She frowned. "I thought I was the only one who knew about the safe. It was hidden inside the wall. You had to know it was there. You couldn't see it by looking around the house."

Fargo frowned at her words. The attacker had been there when she arrived at the house. But he'd found no hidden safe. Perhaps she was right. He wasn't there because of the safe. It fit in its own way, Fargo thought. Perhaps the attacker had come only to destroy the house. That fit, too. The fire had burned too quickly, consuming the entire house too furiously, to have been a last-minute thought turned into action by breaking a kerosene lamp.

"What are you thinking?" Bonnie asked, breaking into his frowning silence.

"About things that don't fit and things that do," he answered.

"That's a nothing answer."

"It's all you'll be getting now," he said. "Tell me, if you didn't like what you found, what were you going to do? Were you going to destroy it to protect his name as you knew him?" Bonnie glowered back but made no reply. "A lot of good that would've done in helping to catch his killer," Fargo said.

"I don't know what I was going to do," Bonnie muttered. "I hadn't thought it through that far. I just wanted to see for myself, just Grandpa and me again, alone. He always let me ask questions, even when he didn't answer." She looked away and her pert face held a little-girl sadness in it.

"Maybe you'll still get a chance to find out for yourself—but not alone." She turned and frowned at Fargo. "I'd guess a safe hidden inside a wall would be cast-iron. It ought to stand up to the fire, probably the only thing that will," he said. "Soon as things stop burning and cool down we'll have a look."

He followed her eyes as they swept the smoldering blackened area where a house had once proudly rested. He wondered if perhaps it wasn't a proper epitaph for Sam Whitford.

"It'll take till morning to cool down enough to go poking about," Bonnie said.

"At least," Fargo agreed, pushing to his feet and walking to the Ovaro. He took his bedroll to the edge of the trees beyond the circle of smoky air. Bonnie slowly walked to him as he set out the bedroll and stretched out on it. She dropped to her knees beside him and managed to look remorseful as well as defensive.

"I didn't expect it to turn out this way," she said. "But you've a right to be angry with me."

"Thanks," Fargo said dryly.

"There's no need for sarcasm," she sniffed. "I was only trying to say I'm sorry, really sorry."

He reached out and pulled her down beside him. "Accepted, girl, for now."

She lay down and studied him. "What's that mean?" she asked.

"It means I won't be accepting any more of it," he said. "Now get some sleep."

"I can't sleep."

"Then catnap," he growled, and closed his eyes. He pulled sleep around himself but heard her tossing restlessly until she finally settled down, her hand closing over his arm.

The remainder of the night stayed quiet; the first pink streaks of dawn had crossed the sky before he snapped awake in the early light. The faint sound of hoofbeats broke the stillness and grew louder. He stayed on the bedroll as his hand drew the Colt from its holster. He was watching the road when Bonnie woke. He put one hand across her mouth. She lay still, her eyes round and wide, with a touch of fear in them.

The horse and rider came into sight, drew closer, took on shape and form.

It was Hal Comager, hatchet jaw thrust forward. Comager reined to a halt in front of the charred, blackened piece of earth and slowly dismounted, took a few steps closer to the charcoal embers, and halted.

Fargo drew his hand from Bonnie's mouth and rose to his feet. "Surprised or satisfied?" he asked softly.

Hal spun, stared in surprise at him. "What the hell's that supposed to mean?" he barked.

"It means maybe you like to play with matches," Fargo said.

Bonnie was instantly at his side.

"You're crazy, Fargo. I didn't do this," Comager flung back.

"How come you weren't in the bunkhouse last night? None of the other hands, either."

"I rode to Axlerod with some of the boys. We have to start looking for work," the man answered.

"Then they can back that up?" Fargo pressed.

The man's brow beetled. "Well, no, we separated, went our own ways when we got there," he answered.

"Convenient."

"It's true, goddammit," Comager half-shouted. He paused, his face taking on slyness. "How do I know you didn't do it? You're here, waiting around."

"He didn't do it, Hal," Bonnie said. "I got here first. I was left to burn in the fire."

Comager shrugged. "Not by me."

"We'll find out," Fargo said.

The man's eyes shot hatred at him. He spun and stalked toward the bunkhouse. "Came by to get some fresh clothes, that's all," he flung over his shoulder, and continued into the bunkhouse.

Bonnie's eyes went to the big man beside her. "You believe that?" she asked.

"It's awful neat," he said. "But believing or not, believing doesn't mean a damn. All that counts now is proof, and we have damn little of that." She fell silent as Comager stalked from the bunkhouse, clothes over his arm, and climbed onto his horse. He threw a glare at Fargo and sent the horse into a gallop, disappearing down the road in the morning's new light.

Fargo stepped toward the charred remains of the house, kicked some of the pieces of ash with his foot, bent down, and brought his face closer to the embers. "It's cool enough," he said. "Let's go look."

He started through the charred cinders and Bonnie hurried alongside him, gesturing to the blackened ground where the master bedroom had been. Fargo saw a smoked piece of plank sticking into the air, obviously leaning on something. He hurried closer. He halted beside the square, small shape and kicked away the plank leaning against it. As he had expected, the safe was iron and had withstood the flames to remain only blackened, a square tombstone. He kicked at it and moved, a cloud of black ash dust rising into the air. It took real effort, but with Bonnie's help, he finally shoved the solid little safe onto the grass nearby.

He drew the Colt, placed the gun barrel against the lock at the front of the safe, and fired two shots that shook the iron box. The door to the safe slowly swung open, and Fargo reached inside, his hand moving across a long ledger. He drew it into the open and cast a glance at Bonnie as she stared at it and swallowed hard. She felt his eyes on her and looked up, anger, fear, pugnacious defensiveness all churning in her round, pert face. He offered the book to her, but she shook her head.

"No," she snapped. "Just get on with it, dammit. Open it. I'm not afraid."

His smile was gentle as he opened the ledger.

5

The neat rows of figures seemed to march across the pages like tiny soldiers in close-order drill. Each page was headed with a name; the figures beneath it listed transactions, dates, and amounts. Fargo turned the pages and gazed down at more of the same neat rows of information. He shot a glance at Bonnie as she stared at the pages with him, her face set tight, but not enough to hide the anguish.

Page after page took them backward in time. He halted halfway through the ledger and flipped to the very back of the book, his eyes quickly finding the dates. He grunted in grim amazement. The pages were a chronicle down through the years, almost seventeen of them. He closed the book and looked at Bonnie. She met his eyes with her head high, her gaze steady, yet he caught the tiny tremor of her lower lip.

"All of it, all the years of it," he said softly. "Everything Carrie told me was true."

She turned away, defeat and pain in her silence. Fargo reached into the blackened iron safe again and pulled out an oblong tin box. He set it on top of the safe and opened it. A half-dozen pieces of paper lay inside. The top one, he saw as he unfolded it, was a deed to the property where the house had stood. Beneath it was another deed to a parcel of adjoining acreage. The third folded piece of paper bore a half-dozen handwritten lines, and as Bonnie stood by, Fargo read the words aloud:

"Be it known to all that on this date, May twelfth, 1839, a girl child was born to Clara and Fred Whitford. Signed, Clementine Paddleton, midwife," Fargo read, and his eyes went to Bonnie. "This is your birth record," he said. "If you're twenty-two years old."

"I am," she said. "What's next?" Fargo opened the last piece of paper and Bonnie leaned forward. "That's Grandpa's writing," she said.

Fargo read aloud again. "It is agreed that I will furnish Clarence Higgins room and board and pay all his living expenses plus a sum of twenty-five dollars a month for the rest of his natural life. For this consideration Clarence Higgins agrees to act for me and to perform all the services agreed upon between us so long as they shall be needed." He halted.

Bonnie, reading beside him, saw that the letter of agreement had been signed by Sam Whitford and Clarence Higgins.

Fargo frowned down at the paper. It was an agreement that said nothing about what it concerned, a bond signed by two men clearly in full understanding of its meaning with nothing spelled out.

"How strange," Bonnie murmured, following his thoughts.

"Who's Clarence Higgins?" Fargo asked.

"I don't know. I never heard the name before," Bonnie answered. "What's it mean?"

"Dammed if I know," Fargo said. "But it's important. It was in the safe with your grandpa's most important, personal papers. It has to be important."

There was a final piece of paper in the tin box, a small, torn scrap with only a few words scrawled upon it: *Clarence Higgins—Deep Valley*. Fargo's eyes narrowed in thought as he closed the tin box. "I know a Deep Valley, wild country at least a week's ride north."

"Maybe we ought to pay a visit," Bonnie said.

"We'll see," Fargo replied. "Meanwhile, we'll take everything back to your place. It ought to be yours anyway."

Bonnie took the ledger and climbed onto the roan while he carried the tin box. She rode back in silence beside him. When they reached her place, she took the things from the safe into the house and he put the horses in the barn. When he returned he found her feeding the Churra sheep, so he went inside and sat down. He let her finish her chores alone, aware of the power of the mundane, the importance of ordinary things to the heartsick soul.

He had a pot of coffee ready when she finally returned. She accepted the mug of hot, bracing liquid and folded herself into a chair, her pert face solemn. "We know it's all true now. One of them did it. They all had a reason," she murmured.

"Maybe," Fargo said.

"How can you say maybe? It adds up. It had to have been one of them," she said.

"Maybe," he repeated. "Its adds up, I'm sure, but maybe not the way we're thinking."

"What do you mean?"

"I keep remembering what your grandpa said when he hired me. It looks as though I'm going to have to do some manhunting, he told me. What does that say to you?" Fargo asked.

"He knew one of them was going to try to kill him and he wanted you to find out who," she said.

"Yes, he knew somebody was after him, but not necessarily Hal Comager, Carrie, Simon Carter, or any of the others." Bonnie frowned at him. "They were all under his nose. He didn't need a trailsman to hunt any of them down. He had to be thinking about somebody else," he told her.

She took his words in with her eyes wide, holding on him. "Yes, I see," she murmured. "Is there anything else?"

"Maybe," he said.

"That means you're not going to tell me what," she sniffed.

"For now. Want to think more on it," he said.

Bonnie finished the coffee and put the mug down. "I'll tell you something else that doesn't fit. The figures in that ledger represented a lot of money over all those years. What'd he do with it? Where'd he spend it? Grandpa was well-off, but he never went around doing rich men's things."

"Maybe he salted it away," Fargo suggested.

Bonnie shook her head. "No. I saw his bankbook a few times. It never showed that kind of money. What'd he do with it? It just doesn't fit."

"No, it doesn't. And neither does another thing."

"You changed your mind about Hal and the others? You saying none of them did it?" Bonnie questioned.

"No," he said quickly. "I'm saying there's enough to make me wonder, and the only answer to wondering is finding out."

"How? You can't go about shadowing each of them. It'd take forever and you might not turn up anything more than we have now: reasons but no proof," Bonnie said.

"When you can't get into the fox's lair, you make the fox come out," Fargo said, and smiled at her frown. "I'll explain as we go along and you'll be a part of it." He saw the reassurance hit home as the determination returned to her face at once. "I'm going to my saddlebag to get some extra clothes," he said. "You have any old rags or sheets we can use for stuffing?"

"Stuffing?" Bonnie frowned.

"We're going to make a rag doll, sort of." He laughed and strode from the house. He returned carrying an extra shirt, Levi's, and jacket. Bonnie had a pile of old rags on the floor and he put the extra clothes down beside her.

"We're going to make a dummy," she said. "Of you."

"Bull's-eye," Fargo pronounced. "You start stuffing. I'll get a piece of log to give the body support."

"I have an old pillow we can use for the head," she said, and hurried off as he went outside.

"Get a needle and thread. We want to make sure everything stays in place," he called back. When he returned, she had already started stuffing the shirt. She halted when the night arrived and made supper of pork chitlins and wheat cakes. They continued working after they finished eating. When they finally stopped, the figure was almost complete, body and legs stuffed and the dummy able to stand by itself, albeit precariously.

"We'll do the rest in the morning," Fargo said, and stretched his long, powerful arms.

"What happens afterward?" Bonnie asked.

"We see which fox comes out of its lair," Fargo said. "Now you'd best get some sleep."

She nodded and rose, pausing beside him. Suddenly her lips were on his, sweet softness, a tender touch to her kiss. "For everything," she murmured as she pulled back and hurried into her room.

Fargo rose and undressed in the small spare room. He stretched out naked on the bed and went over his plans for the next day. Bonnie would be a part of them, of course. He'd need her to help pull it off, but it would also take a combination of two powerful forces—fear and self-protection.

He finally closed his eyes and slept while the moon moved silently across the sky. But he slept as he most always did, with the inner senses awake. His eyes snapped open as he caught the faint click of the door latch. He'd been asleep only an hour or two, he guessed, his hand closing around the Colt at the side of the bed. The door opened and the small figure entered, a shirt hanging almost to her knees.

She came toward the bed and halted beside him, her eyes going over the naked beauty of his muscled body. "I couldn't sleep," she said. "I kept thinking that last night I was almost dead."

"Almost doesn't count," Fargo said gently.

"Suddenly I didn't want to be alone."

"Is that all?" he questioned.

"No." A moment of concession touched her face. "I wanted to be with you. I wanted you holding me. Is that admission enough?" Exasperation tinged her voice.

"It'll do," he said. "Come here." With one knee on the bed she stopped, her eyes drawn to his groin. The gaze lingered and finally returned to his face. He reached up and began unbuttoning her shirt. She remained rigid, her breath coming in quick, shallow gasps. As he reached the last button, the shirt fell from her shoulders, and her breasts tumbled free, beautifully round and firm with tiny pink-brown tips in the center of small, pink circles. She had a young, firm body with round freckled shoulders. A slightly rounded belly pushed from below her waist, and a small but gloriously thick black V rested near her young, firm thighs.

Once again he tasted the tenderness of her lips, softness that grew firmer as they opened hungrily and he explored with his tongue. She murmured eagerly, and when his hands closed around the very firm, high breasts, the sounds became gasped words of delight. "Oh, God, nice, nice . . . oh, so nice," Bonnie murmured. "Yes, press, feel, touch . . . oh, God, yes." Her own tongue darted, entreated, touched his, exchanged silent promises of desire. When he turned her on her back, a long groan of pleasured anticipation arose from deep inside her. He left her mouth, brought his lips to the small brown-pink nipples, and gently enclosed them. Bonnie emitted a hoarse cry of delight, and her fingers dug into the back of his neck.

Her belly lifted, fell back, and her beautiful thighs rose, close together, then turned to one side as his tongue slowly circled the edge of each pink areola—pulled gently, kissed, licked. Bonnie's pert face crinkled in a smile. "Yes, nice, oh, God, so nice . . . so good . . . mmmmmm," she breathed. He tasted the sweetness of her skin, smoothly firm, full of the vigor and vitality of youthful wanting.

She slid her breasts against his chest, moved down to press them into his abdomen and slowly slid their high roundness back to his mouth. "More, more, please," Bonnie whispered, and pressed her left breast into his mouth. Another tiny cry of delight erupted at his touch.

One hand slid lightly over her rounded belly, and he felt it harden, grow soft as she relaxed. His fingers moved down over her thick triangle, pressed into its luscious tangle and down onto the pubic mound that had grown hard. "Oh, oh, oh, God," Bonnie gasped as his fingers slid downward to touch the tip of the dark, moist portal. "Aaaaiiii . . . ah, aaaaah," she cried out, but her thighs still stayed pressed hard against each other. He pushed his hand between their hot firmness. There was a murmur of protest as she held tight, then suddenly her legs came apart, almost slammed closed again, and fell apart once more.

He closed his hand around her and let the moistness seep against his palm. "Jesus . . . oh, my God," Bonnie cried out, but he heard the urging in her voice. As his fingers probed gently, explored, touched the lubricious entrance, Bonnie screamed in pleasure. "Come to me, Fargo . . . oh, come to me."

He lowered himself over her, resting his rigid, throbbing fire against her rounded belly. "Aaaah, ah, ah . . . ah, yes, yes yes . . . oh, yes," Bonnie breathed, turning her head from side to side, arching and offering her young, firm breasts. He bent his face and pulled on them while Bonnie emitted low, groaning sounds. He felt the full, firm thighs come up, press against his sides, fall away, and come back to press again. He slid down a few inches, his burgeoning organ just touching the moist entranceway. Bonnie screamed. With a passionate violence, she pushed herself up and forward, pushed over him with a glorious scream of pure ecstasy.

He slid forward, into the dark, wet corridor, and Bonnie moved with him at once—slowly first, then quickening as he began to increase the motion. She pumped against him, gasping cries of delight in perfect rhythm. She cried out for more with every movement of her body, with every thrust and push, and as he made love to her with increasing roughness, it drew only more sounds of pleasure. Bonnie's young figure bounced with him, the high, round breasts reaching upward for his mouth. Suddenly he heard the short, sudden gasp, and she arched her back, held in midair.

"Oh, God . . . yes, yes, now, now . . . aaaaaah," Bonnie cried. The firmness of her thighs clamped around him, the quick contractions of her warmth enveloping him. She let out a half-cry, half-laugh of pure, passionate delight. Her mouth fell open, her neck arching, her lips forming a smile as the moment of moments swept through her, seizing, commanding, consuming. It was embraced with every part of her body—breasts, arms, belly, thighs—everything shimmering flesh. Even the freckles seemed to dance across the bridge of her nose, and he laughed with her, burying his face into her breasts as her arms clasped around his neck.

When her viselike grip finally fell away, she lay back with a long, satisfied sigh. She smiled at him, a dreamy, almost vacant smile, but her hands moved slowly across his chest. "I didn't intend this to happen," she murmured. "Can you believe me?"

"I can believe you didn't realize you wanted it to happen." Fargo smiled.

She sat up, round breasts thrust deliciously forward, instant belligerence touching her face. But it vanished as quickly as it had appeared, and a small smile edged her lips. "Fair enough," she said. "But I realize what I want now."

"What's that?" Fargo asked.

"More," she murmured, and ran her hand slowly down his muscled torso, tracing a delicate path across his groin and closing her hand around his still-warm maleness. "Oh . . . oh, God," she murmured, turned, and brought her lips to his chest. He felt himself surging, responding at once as she nibbled her way down his body, lips soft as silk, arousing, exciting beyond resistance. Not that he figured to resist, Fargo grunted. His own soft moan of delight broke the stillness as she found him, touched, caressed, silk-soft lips bringing excruciating pleasure. He let her have her way with him, and when she groaned and moaned in her own gratification, he pulled her up onto her back and thrust his eager self into her. She screamed in joy, her arms clasping around his neck, her smooth body pressed tight against him.

She thrust with him, harder and harder each time, quickly now, passions running wild. Finally, with a half-roar, half-laugh, she came with him, a climax of wild and surging abandon. He barely heard her gasped words of delight as she clung to him, then her soft lips found his, pressed hungrily, voraciously into him. When she uttered the final cry of pleasure, she fell back on the bed to offer the same sigh of satisfaction and the same dreamy smile. She lay gathering herself while he enjoyed her vibrant youthfulness, one hand cupping a round, high breast.

"Mmmmmm . . ." Bonnie turned to lie against him. "Maybe this is the only good thing that will come of all of this," she said quietly.

"Maybe," he said. "Be grateful for it, then."

"I am," she murmured. "It's been an education for me. Life is made up of sudden changes. I never realized that before."

"Was this one of them?" Fargo smiled at her.

"I guess so," Bonnie said. "One of the nice ones." She pressed herself tighter against him, found a hollow in his shoulder, and was asleep in moments. He lay awake for a few minutes. Tomorrow could bring as many questions as answers, he realized. This continued to be a thing of sudden turns. And the darkness still lay someplace inside it. He knew it, felt it, something hidden beyond murder itself. How much would touch the pert and defensive young woman in his arms? he wondered. He suddenly realized he was feeling protective. She had her own ways of getting to one, he grunted as he closed his eyes and slept with her.

When morning came he rose, and she finally stirred herself into wakefulness. She sat up, stretched, the round breasts deliciously pulling upward, and Fargo forced himself to turn away. He went outside, drew a bucket of well water, and washed. He went back in and finished dressing. When Bonnie emerged from her room, she was her usual pert, well-scrubbed self in a green blouse and black riding britches.

"A few more touches and he's ready," Fargo said with one hand on the figure that wore his clothes.

"What now?" Bonnie asked.

"We do some visiting," Fargo answered.

"We?" She frowned.

"I'll do most of it. You'll do one. I'll go over it with you, but first, what's a spot around here that's tucked away yet well known?"

"Black Rock Oak," Bonnie said without hesitation. "A kind of landmark for travelers, it's a tall, black rock that sits on a hill with a huge oak behind it. There's heavy brush and other oaks surrounding it, but it's so tall you can spot it from the road a half-mile away."

"Sounds perfect," Fargo said. "Let's go through your part over coffee." She nodded and put the kettle on as Fargo examined the clothed figure again, tried his hat on the pillow head, pulled it low, and turned the collar of the jacket up. It worked, he murmured in satisfaction, the upturned collar touching the jacket, hiding the face that would normally be inside it. It was sure to work at night. "We've got a few touches to put on tonight, but we're about ready to go," Fargo said as Bonnie brought the coffee.

"And I'm still pretty much in the dark," she said with a half-pout on her face. He drew her down beside him on the wood bench and began to explain everything he had planned. She listened carefully, her eyes growing wider as he went on. When he finished and sat back, a wry smile touched her lips. "Getting the fox out of its lair," she murmured. "Ingenious, if it works."

He finished the coffee, rose, and pulled her to

her feet. "You want to go over your part again?" he asked.

"No, I have it, every word of it," Bonnie said.

"Come right back here when you've finished."

She nodded, then stepped to him, her arms encircling his neck, and pressed her lips against his. "For luck," she murmured.

He patted her round rear as he stepped back. He went to the barn, saddled the Ovaro, and rode from the ranch. Bonnie had only one visit to make. He had six, so he sent the horse into a fast trot. He'd decided to begin with Simon Carter. When he drew up in front of the house, it was Ada who came out first, her eyes hardening at once.

"What do you want here?" she pushed at him. The door opened behind her and Simon Carter appeared.

"Got something you might want to know about," Fargo said. The couple waited, Simon Carter's dour face seeming even more despondent than usual. "I know who killed Sam Whitford," Fargo went on. "I know why and when and how."

"Why are you telling us?" Simon Carter muttered.

"Because I'm a reasonable man. Think it over. I'll be at Black Rock Oak tonight at eight o'clock on the dot." Fargo turned the Ovaro around and slowly rode away. Simon and Ada Carter stared after him until he was out of sight, he knew.

His next stop was Abe Floy, who turned out to be on the portly side with a blond-haired wife who echoed his width. A man with small, shrewd eyes that seemed to hide behind the folds of his face, Floy regarded his visitor with hostility.

"I heard about you, Fargo," the man said. "Been

trying to help Bonnie Whitford find her grandpa's killer. Real Good Samaritan, you are."

"So good that I know who did it," Fargo said. "Just the way I know about Sam Whitford's deal with you."

Fargo saw Abe Floy's fat face redden. "You accusing me?" the man spit out.

"I'm just saying I know, and I can prove it," Fargo answered calmly. "But I'm willing to listen before I move on this."

"What's that mean, mister?" Abe Floy questioned.

"It means I'll be at Black Rock Oak tonight at eight-thirty sharp," Fargo said, dug his knees into the pinto, and sent the horse away at a canter. He hurried down the road and out of sight of Abe Floy and his wife, then made his way to the hills where the wood carts, mounds of planking, and entrance holes in the hills unmistakably signified a mining operation. The low house stood at the far end. When Fargo reached it, a tall man with a grizzled, two-day beard and a suspicious eye came outside. "Harry Straker?" Skye Fargo asked. The man nodded. "Name's Fargo."

"You're the one snooping around after Sam Whitford's killer," the man said. "Simon Carter talked to me about you."

"He give you a friendly warning?" Fargo asked.

"I don't need any warning. I didn't kill him," Straker said.

"You had a good reason. He was taking half of everything your mine brought in. He knew it was no accident that killed your partner." Fargo saw surprise flood the man's face first, quickly followed by anger.

"Get the hell out of here, mister," Harry Straker said.

"Just thought you'd like to know that I know who killed Sam Whitford," Fargo said calmly. "I know, and I can make it stick."

"How?" the man snapped.

"That's my business," Fargo said.

"I didn't kill him," Straker said angrily.

"That's what everybody says. But most of the others don't have your reason, Straker. You had the reason, the time, and the chance," Fargo answered. "You want to talk some more about it I'll be at Black Rock Oak at nine tonight." He took in the man's anger, which fairly shimmered from him, turned the horse around, and calmly rode away.

Once past the mining hills he turned the pinto east and quickened his pace. He'd decided to skip Egbert Allcomb. The man's involvement was with Abe Floy, and if there was killing to be done, he wouldn't be the one to do it. But there was Rob Cleaver. Carrie had said that Sam Whitford was an investor in Cleaver's riverboats. Maybe that investment was also based on blackmail and threats. Cleaver had been at the party, so he couldn't be left out. Finally Fargo slowed the magnificent Ovaro as he reached a long, low ranch house with a slate roof and carefully manicured shrubbery encircling it.

He swung from the horse and a delicate blond woman, younger than he'd expected, came from around the side of the house, a basket of cut flowers on her arm. "Looking for Rob?" she asked. "I'm Betsy Cleaver. Can I help you?"

Fargo kept his face cold, his voice flat. "Get me your man," he growled.

A tiny frown crossed her face. "May I have your name?" Betsy Cleaver asked.

"Afterward," Fargo rasped, his face still stony.

The woman nodded, wariness in her eyes, and went into the house.

Fargo stayed on the Ovaro until she returned with a man at her side, well-dressed in a gray silk vest and a ruffled shirt. He was tall, but there was an unmistakable weakness in his face.

"I'm Rob Cleaver," he said with an edge of disdain in his voice.

"The name's Fargo," the Trailsman answered. "I've been after Sam Whitford's murderer."

"A tragedy, but why come to me about it?" Cleaver asked.

"Came to tell you I found the answer."

Cleaver's eyes narrowed, but he held a faintly condescending smile in place. "Good for you," Cleaver said. "I still don't see how this requires a visit to me."

Fargo had chosen his words and had them ready. "I'd say you know that better than I do," he remarked. It was obvious that the man had difficulty hanging on to the smile.

"What are you trying to say, Fargo?" Cleaver asked.

"I'm saying if you dig enough, you come up with reasons nobody else knows about, reasons that'd make any jury convict a man." Cleaver's face had grown hard, his mouth a thin line now. "But I'm a man who's willing to listen." Fargo smiled. "I'll be at Black Rock Oak at nine-thirty sharp tonight." He turned away and felt Rob Cleaver's stare following him until he was out of sight. He had been fishing, Fargo realized, but now he was certain he'd touched on a sore place. He turned the horse back east. He'd only one stop left and that was in Horsehead.

He reached town as the sun began lowering across the afternoon sky; he pulled up in front of the dance hall and went inside. Carrie saw him come in at once from her position at the corner of the bar, and her gaze was both surprised and wary. He walked to where she stood, ordered bourbon, and let her watch and wonder while he wagered with himself how long it would take her to toss questions at him. The wait was only long enough for him to take the first sip of his bourbon.

"You come to drink or to talk?" Carrie asked in a quiet voice.

"Both," he said, sorting his words carefully. She was the most difficult of all, he realized, because she knew the most. "Got some news you might want to hear," he slid at her. "I know who killed Sam Whitford." He took another sip of the bourbon and let his words hang in the air.

"Why tell me?" Carrie asked carefully.

He kept his smile enigmatic, almost chiding. "Thought you'd like to know."

"I told you I have nothing to do with it," Carrie said, her voice growing harder.

"I know what you told me, honey," Fargo said softly, "and I know what I found out."

"I was here the night he was killed."

"Not all night. Nobody saw you for a few hours," Fargo countered.

"I went upstairs and took a nap," the woman hissed. "You're not pinning this on me."

Fargo shrugged. "I'll be at Black Rock Oak to-night, ten o'clock. I'll always listen to a good of-fer." He finished the bourbon and smiled at her.

"Get out of here, damn you," Carrie ordered.

"Whatever you say, honey." Fargo strolled from the dance hall. He rode unhurriedly from town. It was done—all except one, and he'd left that to Bonnie after rehearsing her carefully. He drew a deep sigh and realized he felt the most pity for Carrie. He'd tossed a shot in the dark and it had hit on target. She hadn't been seen at the dance hall through the entire night of Sam Whitford's murder. Maybe she had gone up to take a nap, as she'd said. And maybe not. But he'd be getting answers soon enough, he thought as he rode out of town feeling both sorry and excited.

The ashes that had once been a house blackened the ground; the girl was a lonely figure stepping among the charred remains. She halted before the square iron wall safe, now hanging open and empty, a silent reminder of another world, another person from the one she had known and loved and re-spected all her life. She turned away from it, went to the bunkhouse, and stared in at bunks that were now mostly stripped bare. But Hal Comager's things were still there, as were the possessions of two other hands. She returned to the charred ruin to wait.

The air still smelled of burned wood, Bonnie thought as she drew a deep breath. She found a piece of branch long enough to use as a poking stick and slowly rummaged through the cinders. It helped pass the time, and perhaps she'd find something, she told herself, knowing the thought was empty. But Fargo had told her to wait and she did so, refusing to let the memories flood back on her of a house and a man she had loved. The day had turned into late afternoon when the faint sound of hoofbeats finally reached her ears. She was still standing in the ashes when Hal Comager rode into view and reined up at the bunkhouse, frowning at her. She quickly walked to him and drew a deep breath. "What are you doing here?" the man asked.

"Wasting time, I guess," she said. "I thought I'd poke around and see if I could find anything that might help."

"Can't see that," Hal said.

"You're right. There was nothing," Bonnie said. "Then I decided to wait for you." Hal Comager frowned even deeper at the remark. "You've worked for Grandpa for so long, I feel there's something I should tell you," Bonnie began, then cut off. She seemed to grope for words. "It's about Fargo."

"The hell with Fargo," Comager snapped with instant anger.

"He says he knows who killed Grandpa." Comager's eyes narrowed. "I told him he was all wrong but he wouldn't listen to me."

"He says I did it?" Comager queried.

"He didn't tell me that, but he's talking like that's what he thinks," Bonnie said. "I told him he was wrong. I convinced him to talk to you again and listen to you, let you prove to him that you didn't do it."

"Go on."

"He agreed to that much. He's going to be at Black Rock Oak tonight, ten-thirty," Bonnie said.

"He promised he'd listen to you. If you want to, of course," she added quickly.

"Obliged," the man said.

"I figured you couldn't be the one, not after all these years," Bonnie said. "No matter how angry you were with Grandpa," she added as an afterthought, and Hal Comager's eyes flashed for an instant. She walked to the roan and left as Hal disappeared into the bunkhouse. It had gone exactly as Fargo had rehearsed it with her. She ought to have been pleased, she knew, but she could feel only a grim sadness as she rode back home.

When Fargo reached Bonnie's place at dusk, she was standing in the doorway. "You see Comager?" he asked.

She nodded. "And I feel dirty. I led him on, practically."

"You tossed out the bait, just like I did," Fargo corrected. "It has to be right to work."

"You're saying the one that takes it will be the killer?"

"That's right. The innocent, those who know they've nothing to fear, won't take it," Fargo said. "The guilty one will come gunning to get rid of you. He'll convict himself by that."

"Or herself," he reminded her, and she nodded soberly. "We have a few last things to finish. Do you have some strong, thin string?"

She hurried into her room and returned with a ball of brown moroccan twine that was perfect for the task. He knelt by the dummy figure and tied a long length of the twine around each leg. "You'll be in the high brush behind the oak, holding the end of the string. When you hear a shot you pull. But not too hard."

"I know, just enough to make him go down, right?"

"I'll be below, where I can see the road. Whoever comes might sneak up from any angle. I can't cover them all, but when they leave, chances are they'll hightail it down the road," Fargo said. He rose and looked out into the darkness. "Time to get the show on the road." He carried the figure carefully to the Ovaro.

Bonnie climbed onto the roan and rode beside him at a slow trot. She led the way to Black Rock, a slab of black granite that ended in a jagged top. Behind it, the tall oak rose high, surrounded on three sides with smaller trees and heavy underbrush.

Fargo steered the horses into the thick, back part of the trees, far enough in so they were invisible to anyone looking up from below. With Bonnie carrying one end, he brought the dummy figure to the front side of the tall oak. He leaned it against the tree, put his hat on it, and turned the jacket collar up.

He moved down the low hill and looked up at the figure from the center, the right, and the left, and smiled in satisfaction. It was as though he were looking at himself. He cast a glance at the moon and saw it had reached the early-evening sky.

Bonnie, her face set tight, hurried into the trees with the two lengths of twine. Fargo found a spot a dozen yards away where the grass grew tall yet let him see the road below. He lay down on his stomach. With his Colt in hand—more as a precaution than anything else—he lay still and waited. The minutes seemed to drag by, the clothed dummy against the tree clearly visible under the moon. He lay motionless and suddenly his ears picked up the faint sound of grass being rustled somewhere to his left along the hill.

His body grew taut. The shot, even though he expected it, was a sudden, jarring noise that made him flinch. His eyes went to the tall oak; he saw the figure go down and vanish from view. He brought his gaze to the road below, frowned as almost a minute went by before the man came into sight, a thin figure hunched over the saddle on a horse moving away at a canter.

He let the rider disappear down the road before he rose and hurried to the oak. Bonnie came from the brush to stare at him. "Eight o'clock. Simon Carter," she breathed. "It was him all along."

"Sure looks that way." Fargo marveled at the surprise he felt. "We'll still wait a spell."

"Why?" Bonnie frowned.

"Someone might come wanting to talk. Maybe they'll say something important," he said, and realized the answer was only a half-truth. He was having trouble accepting Simon Carter as the killer. He lifted the figure, put the hat back on again, and adjusted the collar. The bullet hole in the jacket was invisible except when standing alongside it. "We do it again," he said, waiting as Bonnie went into the thick brush before returning to his place in the grass. This time the minutes seemed to fly by, and he lifted his head cautiously when he heard the footsteps coming up the hill. It was eight-thirty and he watched Abe Floy pant up the hillside, a cape around his portly figure. The man approached openly, no attempt at sneaking up.

"I'm coming up there, Fargo," he called. The man advanced another few yards when Fargo saw the cape pull back and the moonlight glint on the gun. Abe Floy fired two shots and the figure toppled over. He tensed, watched, but Abe Floy turned and half-ran down the hill, moving quickly for all his portliness. Fargo waited until he saw Abe Floy ride off down the road, then hurried to the tree where Bonnie appeared, her brown eyes full of unspoken questions.

"Did they both kill Grandpa?" she gasped.

"Hardly, yet it sure looks that way," Fargo answered. "That's the trouble with things. They're not always what they seem to be." He reached down, lifted the dummy, and put it back in place.

"Again?" Bonnie frowned.

"This is getting too interesting to stop," Fargo said. "Besides, we won't know if this is it unless we go on waiting."

She nodded, her pert face tight. He made his way back down the hillside as she went into the brush. When the hour came, he lifted his head. A figure crawled up the hillside, moving on its belly. As it moved closer, it took shape and became Harry Straker. The man crawled with a long-barreled rifle in one hand, and when he halted, he brought the rifle up to his chin, took aim, and fired. This time the figure fell without Bonnie's help. Harry Straker was already running down the hill.

Fargo watched him disappear, then listened to the clatter of hoofbeats in the night. He pushed to his feet and walked to the tree.

Bonnie sat against the trunk, shock on her pert face. "I don't understand," she murmured. "I just don't."

"We'll talk about it later. Meanwhile, let's get things back in shape. This is becoming a very popular spot. We don't want to disappoint anyone." Fargo put the dummy back into its place, adjusted the clothing, and half-pushed Bonnie back into the trees. He turned to his place on the hill and waited, a sense of astonishment churning inside him. He had made a wager with himself when nine-thirty came, and with it, Rob Cleaver on horseback. The man rode up the hill, a variation of Abe Floy's open approach, Fargo noted. When he moved closer, Cleaver turned his horse and Fargo saw the gun in his hand. He fired three shots and the figure went down. Cleaver raced his horse down the hillside and galloped out of sight as Fargo rose and went to the tall oak.

Bonnie was a silent, shocked figure as she helped him set the dummy up again. She stayed speechless and trudged back into the trees. This time Fargo didn't bother to return to the hillside, but shrank back into the thick brush to the left. The moon had traveled another half-hour across the sky when Fargo's eyes narrowed. The figure came up the hillside, a slender waist and the bottled blond hair unmistakable. She approached closer than any of the others before she halted. "Fargo," she called.

He lifted his voice. He was close enough to the tree to sound as though the words came from the figure. "Come on closer," he said quietly.

Carrie's arm came up and the night was shattered by two quick shots. The figure toppled as Bonnie pulled on it and looked at Carrie. She had dropped her arm to her side and stood motionless on the hillside.

"I'm sorry," she said. "I couldn't take the chance you might make it stick." She turned and walked with slow deliberation as she made her way down the hill.

When she was gone, Fargo stood and walked to the tree, leaned down, and put the figure into place again.

"Once more," he said to Bonnie's stare.

She turned and went back into the trees as though she were sleepwalking. He went back to crouch in the brush nearby. Hal Comager was the last of them and Fargo's eyes swept the hill below, waiting to see the hatchet-jawed face come into sight. He glanced up at the moon, watched its slow climb as still no one appeared below. He felt the frown touch his brow as the moon rose past the half-hour point and on toward the high reaches of the midnight sky. But the hillside remained silent and Fargo let another half-hour go by before he stood and called to Bonnie.

She walked toward him. "He didn't come," she said simply. "I'm glad. One of them had faith in being innocent. One wasn't afraid to be accused."

"Seems that way."

"I'm glad it was Hal," Bonnie said. "It helps, somehow." She looked at him, her eyes round. "What does the rest of it mean, Fargo? They all came. Does it mean they all killed Grandpa?"

"No. It means none of them did," Fargo said.

"Then why'd they come to kill you? That's got to mean something."

"It means they were all afraid they might be found guilty. Each one of them knew they had the reason and the opportunity. They couldn't afford to take the chance of being found guilty or let the past come out. Each of them thought they could only breathe safely if I was out of the way," Fargo explained. "But none of them killed your grandpa. You could say they actually cleared one another by trying to kill me."

He turned and stripped the clothes from the dummy. The jacket was old and worn, and now it had new bullet marks. But it was still usable for bad weather, so he folded it into his saddlebag with the rest of the clothes. He retrieved the horses from their hiding place in the woods, and Bonnie rode in silence as they returned to her place.

When he returned from stabling the horses, she was sitting cross-legged on the bed wearing only a shirt, dejection wreathing her face. "It wasn't a waste," he told her. "We learned something from it. And in its own way, it fits."

She tossed him a sidelong glance. "You never were convinced it was one of them, were you?"

"I couldn't be sure, but something kept bothering me and it's all clearer now," Fargo said. "I found Sam Whitford's body. He hadn't just been killed. He'd been beaten, bludgeoned, and knifed. There was hate in that killing."

"But they all hated him, for years," Bonnie said.

"There's hate and there's hate," Fargo told her. "They had the kind you learn to live with or they'd have put a bullet into him long ago. The hate that killed Sam Whitford was something else, dark and deep and burning."

"Such as?"

"I don't know, but it was twisted and full of rage. That's nagged at me from the start."

"What next, then?" Bonnie asked.

"Might be time to go exploring," Fargo remarked.

"Clarence Higgins?" He nodded. "You think he might be the killer?"

"He's got to fit in somewhere, just as that strange agreement has to mean something," Fargo answered.

Bonnie drew a deep sigh and brought her head into his chest. "I don't want to see the dawn, Fargo. Make me forget it all again."

He lay back with her, sliding the shirt over her head, letting his gaze take in the beauty of her luscious breasts and shapely body. She lifted her legs, held them high, and spread them slowly, not unlike the petals of a morning glory unfolding. He stripped off his clothes as she continued to move her legs with slow, sinuous provocation. Naked, he pressed against her, cupped the lovely, firm rear with both hands. She moved her torso, lifted, sought, moaned in anticipation, and gasped sharply when she found him and brought her lips around him. He made love to her again, and when he began to explode inside her, she cried out with the strange, unmistakable sound of pure joy.

Finally she slept beside him, looking innocent, knees drawn up and lying half across his groin. He found himself wondering if it might not be better for her to stay behind. So far she had been touched only by the pain of her grandpa's death, a hurt made of what, not why. And he knew the why could be far worse. That's where the deep and dark hatred lay—someplace hidden, someplace perhaps best left unrealized by her. Maybe he could convince her to let him go on his own, he thought as he closed his eyes, dimly aware that it would be an impossible task. He lay still, as happy as she to embrace sleep.

6

He let her sleep into the morning, enjoying the warm sensuous touch of her body against his until she finally stirred and sat up to rub sleep from her eyes. He swung from the bed.

"How long will it take us to reach Deep Valley?" Bonnie asked.

"At least a week," Fargo told her.

She climbed from the bed and washed in a big porcelain basin of water. "I'll have to get somebody to look after the stock," she said while toweling herself dry.

"Not if you stay here."

"You can't mean that," she said, staring coldly. "I'm going to see it through to the finish."

He shrugged. "Figured as much," he grunted.

"I'll get the Donnen girl. She's stayed here before for me," Bonnie said.

"All right, we'll leave this afternoon. I'm going to town."

He saddled the pinto and rode unhurriedly and reached Horsehead at midday. The trip was partly to let the smithy check a looseness in the horse's right forefoot shoe, but it was also partly malicious enjoyment, he admitted to himself. They all deserved to sweat some more, to live with the fear of retaliation hanging over them. He smiled when he saw the buckboard in front of the general store, Simon Carter alongside it helping to load three bags of groceries into the wagon.

Fargo rode up and halted alongside the buckboard. Simon Carter turned, saw him, and fell back against the rig. His face drained of all color and his mouth fell open as he stared at the big man astride the Ovaro. The veins of his face became stark blue against the now chalk-white skin. His mouth worked, tried to form words, but only a hoarse gasp came out.

"Something the matter?" Fargo asked, and watched Simon Carter's thin form sink to its knees. The man leaned against the front wheel of the buckboard, shaking, his breath deep rasps. Fargo moved the Ovaro forward with a last icy glance at Simon Carter.

He rode on until he reached the dance hall, where he dismounted and walked inside. The main room was still empty, an elderly black man sweeping sawdust into neat piles. "We ain't open yet, mister," he said.

"I know. Came to see Carrie," Fargo said.

"Miss Carrie still be sleeping," the porter said.

"It's a surprise." Fargo smiled and strode past the man and up the staircase. He stopped outside Carrie's room, enveloped the doorknob with one big hand, and turned it. The door opened and he stepped into the room and let the door shut loudly. Carrie sat up with a start of surprise, naked, the slightly heavy breasts swaying as she blinked and brought him into focus. He walked toward her and saw her lips fall open in astonishment.

"My God," she murmured. "My God." But her mind was quick and he gave her grudging credit for that as the words tumbled from her while she stared at him. "It wasn't you," she breathed, comprehension flooding her face. Without makeup, she looked her age, perhaps even a little older, Fargo took note. She swung from the bed, unmindful of her nakedness. "You tricked me," she said breathlessly.

"Bull's-eye," he growled as she started to reach over to a small end table. His hand shot out, a slap, but delivered with all his strength.

The woman arched backward through the air to land on the bed, breasts, arms, legs all seemingly going in different directions as she bounced twice before lying still. Her eyes opened, blinked at him as a tiny trickle of blood seeped from one corner of her mouth.

"I'm sorry," he said, acid on the words. "I just couldn't take the chance you'd forget."

He spun on his heel and strode from the room and let her hear the harsh laugh as he hurried down the stairs. Outside, he walked the Ovaro to the smithy's and waited while the man tightened the shoe, then he finally rode slowly out of town. News would travel quickly, he knew, and they'd all begin to sweat in fear again, and peer into every shadow and wonder if he were coming to pay them back for trying to kill him. Each and every one of them . . . except for Hal Comager. Fargo smiled and enjoyed the satisfaction in the thought.

When he reached Bonnie's place, he saw the young girl with her in the hog pen, so he went into the house and waited until Bonnie finally came in. "It takes a while to show her everything she has to do," Bonnie said. "I'll pack right away."

"Travel light," he said. He went outside, saddled the roan, and had the horse ready when she appeared with a single travel pouch she slung onto the saddle horn. He led the way north at a brisk pace, and when night fell, he found a spot between two hackberry trees to make camp. "We ride hard again tomorrow," he said.

"And make love tomorrow night again," she said.

"Why not?" He chuckled.

Bonnie was waiting with only the long shirt on when he set out his bedroll. She came inside with him and her hands found him at once, caressing, enjoying, rubbing, making tiny noises as he responded to her touch, grew hot and turgid and eager. She brought him to her and made love with a kind of freedom he hadn't noticed before, a combination of tenderness and harsh desire. The night finally echoed with her half-scream and half-laugh of joyous delight. She collapsed against him, arms around his chest, and slept almost at once. She'd promised a week of pleasure and she looked forward to the delight of it. He hoped it wouldn't end in the kind of pain that nothing washes away but he couldn't shake the feeling of something dark and hidden that still waited.

From the first night when he'd found Sam Whitford's beaten and battered body it had been a trail of surprising turns and twists, with something always out of reach, hidden in its own darkness. It still waited. He went to sleep feeling uneasy.

Bonnie made good on her promise as the days went on and they rode north through the wild Montana Territory, the land the Spanish explorers under Cortés had named the land of mountains. The days were filled with solid, no-nonsense riding, the nights with wonderfully wild passion, and finally, the week at an end, he led the way to a ledge that let him scan the territory far to the north. "There," he said, pointing to a deep dip in the land in the distance, the foliage full and lush. "Deep Valley," he said, and led the way forward.

They moved steadily downhill, yet his eyes never stopped sweeping the thick, heavy forest land and the high ridges where the hills rose. He had seen signs of Indians, a wrist band torn off, unshod pony tracks, a broken arrow. This was mostly Assiniboin land, he knew, with some Gros Ventre and Northern Shoshone. For the most part, they were hunting along the flatland and the plains. They would hunt in the thick forest land when the summer neared an end and the deer worked their way from their preferred feeding on black currant, yew, wintergreen, and dogwood to their second choice of sweet fern, serviceberry, bur oak, and birch.

As he led the way downhill, the country grew thicker, the vegetation taking on a lush richness. Finally he halted with Deep Valley only a thousand yards ahead. It seemed an almost impenetrable mass of tangled foliage and closely packed trees.

"God, how can we ever find anyone in there?" Bonnie protested.

"A man lives in Deep Valley, he has a cabin. If he has a cabin, he needs supplies. There was a trading post at the entrance into the valley, used mostly by explorers and trappers. Let's start there," Fargo said, and turned the pinto into a steep trail that finally leveled out to a narrow wagon trail.

He followed the path that led to a low-roofed shack with a trading post sign over the doorway and a row of rainslickers hung on the outside wall. The cabin was bordered by a double row of young, lean saplings. The man that came to the door was as lean as the saplings, an apron wrapped twice around his thin waist, and a long, lined face with shrewd blue eyes.

"Welcome, stranger, whether you come to buy or just talk," the man said.

"Obliged," Fargo said. "Came looking for Clarence Higgins."

"Clarence's place is right down through the center of the valley," the man said. "He should have stopped in a day back. He usually comes by at the week's start, but he didn't show up. If you see him, tell him I've some of that fancy Moroccan tobacco he likes."

"We will," Fargo said, tipped his hat, and turned the pinto down into the valley. He found a deer trail only wide enough to ride single-file so Bonnie fell in behind him. The valley, thick and dense with foliage, swarmed with wildlife. Flights of grouse and bobwhite took wing when they neared, and wild turkey gobbled vociferously on all sides. He glimpsed black bear in the distance, along with mule deer and moose. The softness of the earth told him the valley was crisscrossed with streams. The trail continued deeper through the thick valley forest.

"It's beautiful in here," he heard Bonnie say. "But it makes me shiver."

He made no reply, yet he felt the reality in her words. There was a tangled, clutching, dark feel to the valley that made it seem a primordial place best left to the wild creatures that inhabited it. The narrow trail took a sharp turn to the left suddenly, but directly ahead, Fargo saw the pathway that had plainly been hacked out of the denseness. It was wide enough for Bonnie to hurry alongside him as he moved forward along the cleared passage. A strange silence suddenly enveloped them and Fargo's eyes narrowed when he saw the cabin at the end of the cleared area. A half-dozen chickens wandered back and forth in front of the house, and as they neared, he saw two goats tethered to the side of the house, one a ewe full with milk.

He rode to a halt in front of the cabin and called out, "Clarence Higgins." His eyes were fastened on the doorway that hung open. No one appeared. He caught Bonnie's quick glance. "Stay in the saddle," he said as he swung to the ground, the Colt in his hand. He stepped to the doorway of the cabin and saw two windows let in enough light to make a large, single room a fairly bright place. But as he swept the room with a quick glance, he felt the oath catch in his throat when he spotted the figure in one corner, facedown, a spilled tin basin beside it.

"Bonnie," he called over his shoulder as he crossed the room in three long strides and dropped down beside the man. He pressed his hand to the man's neck and felt a pulse. "He's alive," Fargo said as Bonnie came up and he carefully turned the man on his back. He looked down at a bearded face with a flat nose, a face he guessed had seen some sixty-odd years. A deep gash ran along the top of the man's forehead, but his breathing was regular.

Fargo lifted him and carried him to a palette of wood and blankets in a corner of the room. "I'd guess he was trying to reach the water in that basin and didn't make it," Fargo said. "See if you can find some tea to brew."

Bonnie hurried to a small stove in the far corner of the cabin where an array of bottles, tins, and jars covered a wooden shelf.

"Got some sarsaparilla here," Bonnie said.

"That'll do fine," Fargo replied. He hurried outside to the pinto, rummaged in his saddlebag, and returned with a vial of ointment. "Arrowroot, comfrey, balm, and dandelion," he said. He found a pitcher of water, cleaned the dried blood from the wound, and carefully applied the ointment.

"You think he fell?" Bonnie asked.

Fargo rose and moved slowly around the room before answering. "He didn't fall. If he'd hit his head on something, there'd be blood somewhere," Fargo explained. "Somebody tried to bash his head in. Would've succeeded with most men, but he seems a really tough old bird."

The tea bubbled and Bonnie poured some in a tin cup and forced it through the man's cracked lips while Fargo held his head up. Most ran out of his mouth, but enough found its way down his throat, so Fargo lowered him onto the palette again.

"What now?" Bonnie said.

"We wait, stay the night and maybe more," Fargo said. "And hope we can pull him out of it. More ointment every four hours along with more tea."

Bonnie glanced around the cabin. "If I'm going to spend even one night here I'm cleaning the place up some," she said with a disapproving gaze.

"Good idea. I'll see if I can find anything to give us some answers," Fargo said, and began to systematically search the cabin. He started in one corner, went through bundles of old clothes and rags, poked under cracked tables and boxes, found a large jar and emptied it to discover only packages of cigarette paper, much of it dried far beyond use. "Nothing," he muttered when he'd finished. "Not a damn thing."

Bonnie had used a splint broom to clean the floor. Fargo went outside with the big Sharps and brought down two rabbits, which Bonnie skinned and cut up for stew.

Clarence Higgins continued to breathe, but he lay motionless between life and death. Fargo rubbed fresh salve on his wound and with Bonnie's help managed to get some more of the sarsaparilla tea into him. The rabbit tasted good; exhaustion pulled on Fargo when he'd finished. He brought his bedroll in and put it on the floor, then added fresh ointment to Clarence Higgins' wound before settling in for the night.

Bonnie pressed herself tightly to him, content just to be against his powerful body. "He's got to come around, dammit," she murmured. "He's our last chance."

"What makes you think he's going to tell us anything if he does come around?" Fargo asked. "Especially if he's the one we're after."

"I'll find a way," she muttered with sudden fierceness. "I didn't come all this way to find a dead end."

He held her and said nothing, but wondered if perhaps not knowing would be better for her. She fell asleep quickly and the night slowly passed into the new day. He woke and quickly looked over at the palette. Clarence Higgins hadn't moved, but he was still alive, his breathing stronger.

Fargo rose and dressed as Bonnie woke. He applied another dressing of the ointment while she put on clothes, and he saw that most of the angry inflammation around the gash had disappeared. Bonnie made coffee and Fargo went outside with a pitcher and brought in some rich milk from the goat. Later, he found a stand of wild plums not far from the cabin and brought back enough to complete breakfast.

He and Bonnie saw a small shed behind the cabin; it held tools and shovels, along with a half-dozen tarpaulins and three empty casks. A pile of straw filled one corner and Fargo kicked at it until he had it all cleared away. "Damn," he swore as he saw only a nest of field mice under the straw. "If he's got anything hidden around here, he's got it buried someplace," he grumbled. "Let's pour some more tea into the old buzzard."

He stepped from the shed, Bonnie beside him, turned the corner to go to the cabin, and came to a halt. The bearded figure leaned against one edge of the open doorway, a long-barreled rifle in his hands. "I'll be dammed," Fargo breathed as he stared at the man. Clarence Higgins stared back, his eyes clear, but the hands holding the rifle trembled.

"Who be you?" the man asked.

"We are the ones who've kept your old hide alive," Fargo said.

"What're you doing here?" the man asked.

"Came looking for you," Fargo said. "The name's Fargo . . . Skye Fargo. This is Bonnie Whitford."

Clarence Higgins tried to keep his face expressionless, but Fargo caught the burst of surprise that touched it at the mention of Bonnie's name. "What do you want with me?" the man asked.

"Answers," Fargo said. "I could talk better without that rifle staring me in the face. And I'll wager you don't have the strength to stand there much longer."

Clarence Higgins said nothing, but the strain in his face grew more pronounced. After another moment he lowered the rifle, placing one hand against the cabin wall as he moved back into the house. Fargo and Bonnie followed him inside, where the man had sunk onto the palette, the rifle still on his lap.

"You'd have been dead if we hadn't come by," Fargo said. "You were in a coma. Another day or two and you'd have been dead. The inflammation from that gash was spreading through your head."

"I'm beholden to you," the man replied.

"I'll make some more tea," Bonnie said, and Fargo watched Clarence Higgins' eyes follow the young woman as she prepared the brew, studying her with more than ordinary curiosity.

"Tell us about Sam Whitford," Fargo said.

The man's eyes went to him, a flash of wariness in the quick glance. "Don't know any Sam Whitford," Higgins said.

"We saw the agreement between the two of you. Don't lie to us, old man," Fargo growled.

Clarence Higgins brought a narrowed stare to him. "You want to know about that? Ask Sam Whitford," he muttered.

"Sam Whitford's dead, murdered," Fargo said, and watched the man's eyes widen in surprise.

"Goddamn," Higgins breathed. "Goddamn." He stared off into space for a moment, suddenly surrounded by his own thoughts.

"Tell us about the agreement," Fargo said as Bonnie brought a tin cup of tea to Clarence Higgins.

The man took it, sipped quickly, his eyes meeting Fargo's waiting stare. "Nothing to tell," Higgins said. "It was between us, that's all."

"Why was he paying you? What were you doing for him?" Fargo questioned.

"He's dead. It's over. I've nothing more to say on it," Higgins answered, and took a deep draft of the tea.

"The hell you don't," Fargo snapped.

Bonnie's voice cut in. "Grandpa went away once a month. It was you he came to see, wasn't it?" she said.

"I don't know anything about it. I'm obliged for your helping me, but you can just get out now," the man said.

"I'm not going anywhere till I get some answers," Bonnie said.

"My head's hurting something terrible. I've got to sleep some more," Higgins said.

Fargo saw the pain that seized the man's face as he lay back on the palette, and decided Higgins was telling the truth, but only about that. "We can wait," Fargo said.

Higgins fought to keep the sudden attack of drowsiness at bay for another moment. "Leave here," the man breathed. "Take her and leave." His eyes fell shut and he was asleep at once, but his words hung in midair, a warning. Fargo caught Bonnie's frustrated stare and motioned for her to follow him outside.

"What's he holding back?" She frowned when Fargo folded his big frame atop a tree stump.

"It's more than holding back," Fargo said. "I don't know what it is, but it's more than that."

"You think he did it?" Bonnie asked.

"No," Fargo said without hesitation. "The surprise in his eyes was real when I told him your grandpa was dead. But more than that, he's a frightened man if I ever saw one."

"Of what?"

"Maybe of whoever almost killed him . . . We'll try another angle when he wakes up."

Bonnie leaned against him and stayed close as the morning turned to noon. When he heard noises from inside the cabin, Fargo rose. Bonnie hurried back with him to see Clarence Higgins at the tea kettle, the rifle still in his hands. He spun, still unsteadily, but brought the gun up at once.

"Damn, you still here?" the man rasped.

"I told you we'd wait," Fargo said.

"And I told you to get out of here with her," the man shouted. Once again, his tone held something more than a command, almost a note of despair in it, Fargo sensed. He seemed unduly concerned with Bonnie's safety.

"Who bashed your head in and left you for dead?" Fargo asked.

"Some dry-gulcher passing through," Higgins said.

"That must be a constant danger. So many people pass this way." The man glared at him. "Try again," Fargo growled.

"I told you, I don't know. He sneaked up on me," Higgins said. "I'll be all right, now. There's no need for you to stay around. Besides, I don't like women around my place."

It was there again, Fargo noted, the emphasis on getting Bonnie away. "That agreement you had with Sam Whitford, tell us what it meant. Then maybe we'll go our way."

"It's done with. He's dead. There's nothing to say about it," Clarence Higgins replied doggedly.

"Then we stay until you decide to talk," Fargo said.

"No, you're taking her out of here," the man said, and raised the rifle. "By God, mister, I'll shoot you if I have to."

Fargo half-shrugged. "Guess you're not a man to change your mind," he said, and took a step back.

"I'm not," Higgins snapped.

"Then there's no point in our staying."

Anger spiraled in Bonnie's face as she stared at Fargo with disbelief. "There certainly is. We can't just leave. I won't," she said.

Fargo took her arm and pulled her roughly with him as he started out of the cabin. "I'm leaving and you're coming with me," he said, and yanked her outside. "Shut up, dammit," he hissed in her ear as he pulled her to the horses. Her fury subsided a little. "Get on your horse and don't argue about it," Fargo ordered. Still glaring, she climbed onto the roan as he mounted the pinto. He rode slowly away, certain that Clarence Higgins was watching from the cabin window.

"Do you want to tell me what you're doing?" Bonnie hissed as she rode beside him.

"Preventing something from happening that won't do him or us any good," Fargo said. "I told you, he's a frightened man."

When they'd gone down the path far enough, he

turned the horse into the thick foliage and moved back toward the cabin in the dense and tangled brush. He dismounted when he'd gone a dozen yards back, and with Bonnie at his heels, he went the rest of the way on foot and halted when the cabin came into sight. He sank down on one knee, his eyes riveted on the hut.

"I don't expect it'll be a long wait," he said to Bonnie. He had hardly uttered the words when Clarence Higgins emerged from the cabin carrying two traveling sacks and his rifle. He disappeared behind the house and reappeared astride an old gray gelding with a white mane, the rifle tucked into a saddle holster.

Fargo waited till the man was opposite where he kneeled in the thick foliage before he rose, moved on quick, silent steps, and pushed into the cleared pathway. "I'll take the rifle first," he said softly, and saw Clarence Higgins spin in the saddle, astonishment in his gray-bearded face.

"Damn you, mister," the man said.

"The rifle," Fargo growled as Bonnie emerged from the trees beside him. Clarence Higgins slowly drew the rifle out and let it drop to the ground. Bonnie picked it up and emptied the shells from it. "Turn around. We're going back," Fargo said. "Get the horses," he said to Bonnie, and she hurried away.

Fargo walked behind Higgins for the short distance to the cabin, watching as the old man unsaddled the gray horse. Bonnie appeared with the roan and the pinto.

Higgins dragged his two traveling sacks back into the cabin and fastened Fargo with a glance that held a kind of sadness. "You're making a bad mistake, Fargo," he said.

"I'll decide that after you tell us about the agreement with Sam Whitford," Fargo said.

Higgins sank down on his palette, the resignation in his eyes joined by a dogged truculence. "There's nothing to tell. It's done with," he said.

"We've got time, old man. We'll stay until you decide to open up," Fargo said. "It's a right cozy place you have here. Bonnie will enjoy fixing it up. Maybe she can make some curtains for the windows."

Clarence Higgins glared at him. "I like my place just the way it is. You take her and get the hell out of here," he persisted.

"Soon as you start telling us what we came to find out," Fargo said.

Higgins looked away, dogged grimness settling into his face.

"You want to start getting supper ready, Bonnie?" Fargo said.

"Yes. I have enough rabbit left over and I saw some wild onions and green amaranth outside that'll add real flavor to it," she said, and strode from the cabin.

Fargo put the rifle in one corner of the room and settled down across from the palette. "Don't even think of trying to get away, Higgins," he said.

The man cast a dark look his way and lay full out on the palette. He was a tough and stubborn old bird. Whatever he was afraid of didn't shake that out of him, Fargo noted, and a frustrated sigh escaped him.

Bonnie returned in minutes with the greens and set out getting the meal ready. When darkness came, she began to dish it out. "You've got to eat, Clarence," she said. "Come to the table."

The man waited a moment, then drew himself up from the palette and sat down at the table. "Damn you, girl, it smells too good for a hungry man to pass up," he muttered.

Bonnie sat down across from him and ate as she enjoyed the way Clarence gobbled up the meal. When he finished, she looked across the table at him and her voice was soft. "Talk to us, Clarence. What's it all about? What does it all mean? Do you know who killed Grandpa?"

"Leave here. Please," Higgins said, despair in his voice.

"Talk and we'll go," Fargo cut in harshly.

The man rose from the table and walked to his palette, sat down atop it with his back against the wall, a gesture of refusal.

Bonnie shrugged helplessly at Fargo as he began to help clear away the dishes.

"Hold steady," he whispered to her. "I'm betting he'll crack open sooner or later. Maybe it'll take another day or two, but he'll crack."

She shrugged again, her eyes telling him she wasn't as convinced as he.

The darkness closed into the cabin and Fargo set his bedroll out, waited, and felt Bonnie against him minutes after. Her arms encircled his chest, one soft thigh half across his legs.

"Tomorrow night we sleep outside where we can make love," she grumbled. "Even if we have to tie him up."

"All right," Fargo smiled.

In minutes Bonnie was fast asleep, her breathing

hard and even. He lay awake a little longer but finally let slumber sweep him up also.

The night had grown deep when he woke, the sounds quickly reaching that inner consciousness that, like the bobcat, never truly slept. He saw Clarence Higgins standing by the palette, watched the man move. But Higgins didn't go toward the corner and the rifle. Instead, he walked to the bedroll. Fargo closed his hand around the Colt that lay at his side. Clarence Higgins halted alongside the bedroll and saw Fargo's eyes open, fixed on him. He put a finger to his lips in a gesture for silence and moved toward the door. Fargo carefully slid Bonnie's arms from around his chest and pushed out of the bedroll and pulled on trousers. Bonnie moaned and turned on her side but stayed fast asleep as Fargo followed the older man out into the night.

"You won't leave, damn you," Higgins said, his voice hardly more than a whisper as he halted a half-dozen yards from the cabin. "And I won't tell it in front of her. We've spent a lifetime, Sam and I, keeping it to ourselves."

"Keeping what to yourselves?" Fargo asked.

"All of it, all the rottenness and sickness in it," the man said. "Fred's a dead man to her. I'm still going to try to keep it that way."

"Fred? Is he the man that tried to kill you?" Fargo questioned.

"Yes, he just showed up a few days ago and came at me. I understand why now. He killed Sam. I guess he figured I had to go, too." Higgins paused, frowned into space as he reflected aloud. "Never thought he'd do that. Guess you can't figure a man who's crazy. You never know when they'll snap altogether."

"Who the hell is this Fred you keep talking about?" Fargo asked.

"Fred Whitford," Higgins said, and Fargo felt the sudden shock stab deep into him, a growing comprehension that turned his stomach. The birth certificate in the midwife's handwriting blazed like a sudden fire inside his mind.

"Be it known to all that on this date . . . a girl child was born to Clara and Fred Whitford. . . ."

"Bonnie's father?" Fargo heard the horror in his own voice.

"That's right," the man said. "Sam Whitford's son. He was a crazy killer then and he's crazier now. The girl's folks didn't die. Fred Whitford killed her mother in one of his crazy rages. The truth was kept from her then and ever since."

"Jesus," Fargo breathed. "How?"

"Only Sam Whitford knew his son had killed his wife. Maybe a lot of what's happened is just Sam's fault, but Fred was his only child. Sam couldn't turn him over to be hung. But he also knew that if Fred stayed with the little girl, sooner or later he'd do something to her, attack her, ruin her life, maybe kill her one day. He made a bargain with his son. I guess you could say rightly that it was a bargain made in hell and sealed by the devil."

"He agreed to pay his son to disappear and never to go anywhere near Bonnie again," Fargo ventured, and Higgins nodded gravely.

"That's right. He never wanted to see his son again. He wanted him dead, but he didn't have the courage to really do it. So all these years he paid

Fred Whitford a handsome sum every month, Satan's ransom, I always call it," Higgins said.

"That's where you came in. You were the go-between. Sam Whitford delivered the money to you and Fred picked it up. That way he never had to face his mad spawn," Fargo murmured with a terrible awe. "That's what was never spelled out in the agreement between you."

"Understood but never spelled out." Higgins nodded. "Sam never wanted a trace of the truth to be found."

"It all fits now," Fargo muttered. "All the monies he took in by blackmail and threats, it all went to pay Fred Whitford to stay away, to stay dead."

"It was wrong, all of it, but it was Sam's way of trying to protect Bonnie, not only from knowing that her father killed her mother, but to keep her safe," Higgins said. "Only now it's all blown apart. Fred's gone off the deep end altogether and killed his pa, too."

Fargo saw the beaten, battered, and knifed form of Sam Whitford in his mind. It all fit down to the last piece, the kind of dark and twisted hate he had felt all along.

"Sam never wanted the girl to know any of it. Maybe that can still be," Higgins said.

"If somebody can get to this maniac before he gets to her," Fargo said. "And he will come after her again. He's plainly on a killing spree." He paused, his eyes staying on Higgins. "You have any idea where he is?" he asked.

"Still in the valley, I'd guess. It was only a few days ago that he came after me. He used to camp due north when he'd come visiting to get his money."

"You have an idea what he did during all those years? Or where he went?" Fargo asked.

"He went all over the country. He had the money for it," Higgins said. "Though he never said exactly where. But sometimes he'd brag about the women he raped and the men he killed."

"I'm going after him," Fargo said.

"By God, be careful. He's a mad dog. He's no old man. He's not more than forty and he's an ace woodsman. He's smart and vicious, and most of all, he enjoys killing," Higgins said. "What'll I tell the girl if you go? I'm not telling her the truth, not after all these years. But I'll have to tell her something she'll buy."

Fargo thought for a moment. "She's a sound sleeper. Chances are she won't wake till morning. You tell her that I heard sounds in the night and got up to find a rogue grizzly near the cabin. You can tell her the bear's been raiding for months. Tell her I went after it so it wouldn't come back and take us by surprise. Tell her just to wait until I come back."

Higgins gave Fargo a thoughtful glance. "What if you don't?" he asked.

"Then take her and run," Fargo said. "But give me a few days, at least."

"I'll see to it," the man said.

Fargo returned to the cabin, dressed in silence, and paused to take another look at Bonnie's sleeping form, her pert, freckled prettiness holding its own special kind of goodness and trust. She deserved not knowing of a bargain fashioned out of terrible wrongs to do good. There were things better left unknown, maybe for all of us, he reflected as he strapped on his gun belt. Clarence Higgins watched him go, his face a mixture of relief and apprehension.

Fargo purposely rode by night. The valley was too thick and dense to pick up a trail even by day. He had to find another kind of trail as he followed the path of the moon northward. It was slow riding through the thick vegetation, much of it tangled vines that were suddenly very appropriate. When dawn came, he halted under a tall bur oak with good sturdy branches and climbed high enough into the tree to look across the valley. Most of the movement he saw was made by wildlife, the sudden motion of leaves from a running herd of deer, the flurry of brush from birds, the slow swaying of branches as a heavy moose lumbered past. But at the far end of the valley he thought he detected a tiny spiral of smoke. It was too far away to be certain, but he shimmied down from the tree and rode north again.

Negotiating the terrain to the far end of the valley took the entire day as the Ovaro had to walk most of the way, picking his legs up high to step from tangles of vines and walking carefully across brush so thick it clutched at the horse's legs. Fargo halted twice to let the horse drink at streams, and it was dusk when he reached the far end of Deep Valley. But unlike most times when the dark made trailing impossible, he welcomed the night and settled down in the twilight to catch a few hours' sleep. When he woke, the moon was high in the sky and he sent the pinto forward through the pitch-black forest.

But seeing wasn't important—not yet—and he rode with his neck arched backward, his head held high for every night scent to come into his nostrils. He'd ridden perhaps another half-hour when he pulled the horse to a stop. The scent drifted to his nose, unmistakable, hickory burning with perhaps a piece of pine mixed in—the scent of a campfire, directly ahead.

Fargo dismounted and left the Ovaro to move forward on foot, steps silent as a cougar on the prowl. The soft glow of light drifted through the tangle of branches as he crept closer to the small campfire, eyes narrowed, but he saw no figure beside the low light. His hand rested on the butt of the Colt on his hip as he took another step closer to peer into the darkness just beyond the glow of the fire. But still he saw no one. The sudden stab of alarm hit into him just as the voice cut through the silence.

"Drop the gun, mister," it said, almost directly at his back.

Fargo straightened, let a deep sigh of anger at himself come from his lips, and dropped the gun to the ground.

"Walk, over to the fire."

Fargo pushed out of the trees into the small cleared space. He turned as the man emerged behind him, his Colt in one hand and a five-shot Smith & Wesson army pistol in the other. Fargo looked at a man of medium height, hatless, a shock of unruly brown hair across his forehead, an angular face with a small scar along his neck. Only his eyes distinguished him from the ordinary man. A bright blue, they seemed to glow with a strange light that gave them a wild, ghostly glare. Bonnie's looks all came from her mother, Fargo decided.

before he rose. When he'd finished dressing, she opened her eyes and her hand reached out to touch his as he stood beside the bed. "You can come again anytime, Fargo," she murmured.

"I might do that," he said. "Thanks for the explanation." She smiled and closed her eyes. He made his way down the stairs, through the empty dance hall, and let himself out a side door. He was still tired, he realized as he rode across the hills. He found a thick bur oak and curled up under it for another few hours of solid sleep. When he rose, the sun was moving toward the noon sky, so he sent the pinto toward Bonnie's place. But as he rode, he wrestled with how he'd tell Bonnie what he had learned. He had to tell her, but there was no easy way, not with her loyalty and defensiveness. He continued to turn things in his mind, and by the time he reached Bonnie's place and saw her come out with a glower on her face, he decided that perhaps the hardest way was the best way. Sometimes harshness was kinder than an attempt to be gentle.

"You've been gone long enough," Bonnie stated coldly.

"Been learning things," Fargo said.

"For pleasure or for business?" she sniffed.

"Maybe some of both," he said blandly. Her mouth tightened. "I could use some coffee." He followed her into the house and leaned against the puncheon table while she poured a tin cup of coffee and handed it to him, then took one for herself. She had put on a crisp white shirt, the two top buttons open so the high swell of her breasts was clearly visible.

"Saw you coming before it got dark," the man said. "Who are you, mister?"

"Friend of your pa's," Fargo answered.

The man's face suddenly seemed to break apart in a wild grimace, lips drawing back, the ghostly wild eyes growing wilder. "Don't lie to me, you bastard. He couldn't send you after me. He's dead," the man shouted.

"He sent me," Fargo returned calmly.

Fred Whitford flew into another explosive rage, and his face contorted again, his mouth working to take in gulps of air. "I'm going to kill you, whoever you are. For lying to me and for saying his goddamn name in front of me," the man thundered.

Fargo moved backward, stepped around the small fire to the other side, and the man moved almost to the edge of the smoldering flames.

"But not all at once, mister. I'm going to kill you in pieces so you can watch yourself die," Fred Whitford said, and he smiled, a gargoyle's grimace. "First your kneecaps, then your ankles. Then your elbows, your hands next, then your balls. Before I'm finished, you'll be begging me to kill you. Now you going to tell me who sent you?"

"God, maybe. I'm not sure. Maybe your wife. Pick anybody," Fargo said.

Fred Whitford let out a scream of rage, his body shaking in a paroxysm of fury. He waved the gun wildly in his rage and smiled grimly. "You bastard. You bastard," the man screamed. "Who are you?"

"Does it matter?" Fargo said.

"Your name. Give me your goddamn name," Fred Whitford roared.

"The man who had to come," Fargo said, and

Fred Whitford screamed in fury again. His ghostly blue eyes seemed to burn.

"You're dead, you're dead," Fred shouted, and again the gun waved.

"I'm a churchgoing man. Mind if I pray?" Fargo said, and dropped to his knees at the very edge of the embers.

"Yes, yes, I'd like that." Fred Whitford laughed, the sound a hollow, wild peal of insanity that rose into the trees. "Pray, go ahead, pray."

Fargo lowered his head but only enough to let him see the gun in the man's hand. "I do not pray for myself, oh, Lord," he began. "I pray for this mad son of Satan before you."

"No, stop that," he heard Fred Whitford shout.

"I pray you will show him no mercy, that you will punish him forever," Fargo went on.

"No, damn you, stop it, stop it," the man screamed, and his hand waved the gun again.

But Fargo was ready, his every muscle tensed. His hands opened on the ground, dug into the edge of the hot ashes, and flipped them into the air as he ignored the pain of his fingers. He saw the man half-turn aside as the ashes flew into his face.

"Goddamn." Whitford coughed, started to turn back with one hand still pawing at his face. But Fargo was already diving, hurtling himself across the low fire like an airborne log. He smashed into Fred Whitford at the knees and the man went down firing the gun into the air. As he hit the ground, he lost control of the pistol and it skittered across the ground.

But the maniac rolled and Fargo felt the wild strength in the man as the figure tore from his grasp. The man pushed to his feet, aimed a kick into Fargo's face that the Trailsman avoided only by a fraction of an inch. Fargo caught at the man's foot, got enough of it to pull, and Fred Whitford slammed down on the ground again. This time Fargo was on his feet first, and as the madman started to rise, he smashed a tremendous right into the man's jaw. Whitford fell back, went down on one knee, and came up, his jaw hanging brokenly. But the man charged and Fargo set himself, threw a powerful left hook that smashed into the broken jaw. Whitford screamed but there was more maniacal fury than pain in it. He slammed into Fargo, his hands closing around the big man's throat.

Fargo put his hands around the man's wrist and tried to pull his grip free, but Whitford's fingers were like a steel vise, locked into place by an inner fury that went beyond all normal strength. Fargo felt the breath begin to leave his throat as he drove both fists into the man's stomach. Whitford grunted in pain and dropped to his knees, but his grip failed to loosen. Fargo stared into the wild, burning blue eyes. The maniac was beyond pain, beyond feeling, consumed with a fury beyond all normalcy. But the air trickling through Fargo's larynx was almost at an end. The Trailsman brought his arms up and Whitford rose to his feet, but the grip of death stayed. The man was past feeling but not past the inexorable laws of balance and leverage. Fargo brought his hands up, closed them around the man's arms, and using all the power of his calf muscles, flung himself backward in an arching half-somersault.

He hit the ground, his body arching upward in the first part of the back somersault, and the maniac's smaller, lighter body sailed over his head, the man's hands tearing from around his throat. Whitford gave a gurgling cry as he went through the air and landed on his back. He started to roll and push to his feet, but Fargo was driving forward and came down with both knees onto the man's chest. He heard the sound of bone shattering as he fell away, rolled, and pushed to his feet. In astonishment, he saw the madman rise, blood pouring out of his mouth, one hand grasping his shattered breast bone. But he half-fell, half-dived for the gun on the ground, only inches from his hand. Fargo stared at him, saw his fingers close around the gun and the bent figure turn to him.

He flung himself sideways as Whitford fired, kept rolling as another two shots followed, all wide of the mark. He got up on one knee as Whitford came toward him in a lopsided, trundling gait, one hand held to his chest. The stream of red continued to bubble out of his mouth. He raised the gun again, driven by the strength of madness, and Fargo dived to the side again as the gun barked twice. He came up on his feet to see Fred Whitford start to turn, take a last limping step, and fall forward. He had the gun pointed at an angle as he fell and his body landed atop his hand. Fargo heard the final shot, a muffled sound, and the madman's body jerked convulsively and lay still.

It was over. Fargo rose and walked to where the Colt lay a dozen feet away. The last of the bargain had been sealed and he felt no sense of victory, not even of relief, only a sour taste in his mouth. He walked slowly past the fire, avoided looking at the still form, as if looking might in some way acknowledge something that was best left forever in a void.

He walked to the Ovaro, slowly pulled himself into the saddle, and realized his neck still throbbed in pain. He rode slowly through the darkness, finally halted, and found a few hours of sleep. He went on again when dawn broke, and the sun was almost at the noon hour when he reached the cabin.

Bonnie came flying from the house and clutched at him as he dismounted, her eyes wide. "I was so afraid when you didn't come back," she said. "Did you get him?"

"Yes," Fargo said, and her head rested against his chest.

"He was a rogue, Clarence said, a mad bear," she murmured.

Fargo's eyes met Clarence Higgins' gaze as the man looked out from the doorway of the cabin. "Yes, he was," Fargo said, and held her to him. "A mad beast." Clarence Higgins turned back into the cabin and Fargo stroked Bonnie's brown hair gently. "But it's over. We can go now," he said.

"Go?" She frowned at once. "But we haven't learned anything yet?"

"Yes, we have. Clarence spoke to me before I left to go after the bear," he told her. "The man who killed your grandpa had been blackmailing him for all his life. Clarence was the go-between. That was the agreement."

"Then we still have to get him," Bonnie said.

"No, he's dead," Fargo said, and she frowned.

"Dead?" she echoed.

"That rogue bear killed him," Fargo said. "I found what was left of him when I killed it. Things work out strangely sometimes. Fate, justice, whatever you want to call it." She stared at him, taking in the import of what he'd told her. "Get your horse," he said. "We're going back."

She nodded, got her things, and climbed onto the roan.

Clarence Higgins watched through the window as she rode away with him.

"It all seems sort of anticlimactic, somehow," Bonnie murmured.

"It turns out that way sometimes," Fargo said blandly, and reached out, put a finger under her chin, and turned her pert face to his. "I'll make it up to you," he said.

"Promise?" She smiled.

"Promise," he said, and watched the freckles dance on the bridge of her nose.

LOOKING FORWARD!
The following is the opening
section from the next novel in the exciting
Trailsman series from Signet:

The TRAILSMAN # 82
MESCALERO MASK

*1861, where the Pecos flowed
from New Mexico into Texas with
the blood of dreamers and fools,
good men and bad. . . .*

The long, powerfully built bronzed figure lay flattened on the rock, clad only in a breechclout. Long jet-black hair held in place by a Mescalero brow band, his eyes were narrowed to little more than slits as he peered at the three blue-clad cavalry troopers sitting quietly atop their mounts. The soldiers, their yellow-gold scarves bright under the hot sun, were positioned on a ledge that commanded a sweeping view of the terrain. The near-naked figure half rose, a tight smile edging his lips. He had already taken note of the other three troopers similarly positioned a quarter of a mile to the west and knew there were another three a quarter-mile to the east.

They had all been put in place. The chief of the soldiers at the fort had a plan, and the big man's lips curled with disdain. He stood straight, the sun glistening on his bronzed skin as he faded back into the crevices of the rock formation to his rear. The pinto he had closeted there gave a quick snort as he approached, and he climbed onto the horse and felt the warmth of the animal's hide against his thighs. He circled slowly down through the rocks, skirting sandstone pinnacles, and when he reached the flat ground where the three troopers would see him he put the pinto into an easy gallop.

It took only moments for two of the three troopers to wheel their sturdy red-brown army mounts, leave the ledge, and race down after him while the third one stayed in place. They would sweep in behind him, and try to chase him into the area covered by the next three troopers. Once there, two of those three would race down to join the chase. He had seen them attempt the maneuver before, and he snorted in contempt as he raced on. The other times, other Mescalero had quickly fled and left the soldiers thinking their tactics had succeeded. This time he would show them better, the hard way.

Glancing back, he saw the two troopers had reached the flat land and turned to give chase. He made a sharp, swerving dash into the jagged sandstone rocks that rose high on his left and kept the horse running hard through the narrow, twisting passage. The two troopers would follow, of course, but they'd have to go single file after him through the narrow passage. He spurred the pinto forward. When he saw the high rock ledge appear, he stood on the horse's back, and gave the animal an extra push with his feet as he leaped upward. His fingers clung and found a grip. He pulled himself up on the rock, instantly swung around on his stomach to lie flat on the ledge.

The two troopers came into sight, one a few yards ahead of the other, chasing the sound of the pinto as it ran on through the passage. The Mescalero let the first trooper race by, half rose, and measured distance as he gathered his muscular body. He held another moment, poised, and when the second trooper passed directly below, he leaped through the air, not unlike a bronzed lance of flesh and blood. He hit the trooper across the back and clung there as the soldier toppled from his racing horse. He was still atop the man as he hit the ground hard. The soldier lay still. The tall, bronzed figure rose, turned the trooper on his side to see a young, unlined face, stunned into unconsciousness but very much alive.

The Mescalero rose quickly. By now the soldier's companion had found the pinto, and he'd have turned in the narrow passage and be charging back. The thought had barely flashed through his mind when he heard the hoofbeats racing down the passage. Moving on quick, lithe steps, the Mescalero went to the trooper's mount and drew the rifle from the saddle holster, a standard army-issue Remington.

He was waiting just in back of the horse when the other soldier raced into view and had to pull back sharply to avoid crashing into the first horse. When he recovered from his surprise, he found himself staring into the barrel of the rifle. He swallowed hard and the Indian's gesture was clear enough. The soldier swung down from his horse and, at another gesture from the powerful, near-naked figure, he turned around.

The sharp blow was just hard enough to send him crumpling to the ground, and with a harsh sound the Mescalero tossed the rifle onto the trooper's unconscious form. He hurried up the passage, retrieved the pinto, and swung onto the animal's bare back. He brought the two army mounts back down through the passage with him, kept hold of their reins as he started across the flat land. He rode at a trot until he reached the place where the next three soldiers were in position to watch over another section of the land. When he caught sight of the three cavalrymen atop their place of observation, he spurred the pinto into a gallop and pulled the two army mounts along behind. He made a wide swing as he raced with the two riderless army horses, and saw the three soldiers straighten up in their saddles. Two instantly swung their horses into action and began to race down after him. But he continued his wide swing that brought him around to the rear of the rocks, and he suddenly swerved into a passage amid the sandstone. He halted, dropped the reins, and let the two army horses come to a stop. He left the mounts at the mouth of the passage and raced the pinto upward. He was deep into the rocks before the two troopers halted at the horses.

He moved quickly through the rocks, swerving from one short passage to another until he yanked the pinto to a halt and leaped from the horse. He climbed on foot through the small spaces between the rock and came out a dozen yards behind the third soldier. The man's attention was riveted on the land below, searching for the two troopers that had gone in pursuit. The tall, bronzed figure moved noiselessly across the open space, long arms swinging loosely. The trooper neither heard nor sensed him until a long arm came up, yanked him from the saddle, and circled his neck. He managed to utter only a strangled gasp until his breath was shut off and he slumped to the ground unconscious. The Mescalero's black hair swung from side to side as he scrambled back across the rocks and returned to the pinto. He rode the horse higher into the rocks until he reached a place that let him look back and down. He halted, waited, and saw the other two troopers find the third one still unconscious on the ground.

He stayed, his eyes narrowed, and watched the two troopers revive the third one. Slowly all three made their way down through the passages and pulled the two riderless mounts along. They disappeared from view as they wound their way downward and came into sight again when they reached the flat land. He saw them turn back and slowly begin searching for the soldiers who belonged to the riderless mounts. A grim smile edging his lips, the near-naked figure rode slowly down the back side of the sandstone formations. The six troopers would return to the fort bruised and battered and more than a little grateful they still lived, he knew.

He rode in a long circle, sent the pinto up a low rise to ride parallel to a long line of shadbush that covered most of the rise. He edged closer to the trees, slowed as he caught the movement inside the brush, and quickly turned the pinto into the shadbush. The foliage moved again, some twenty yards ahead of where he had stopped, and his eyes narrowed as he saw the horsemen appear and halt at the edge of the trees. Six, he counted, all Mescalero, all wearing brow bands and gray, loose-sleeved shirts, some with cut-down Levis, others bare-legged. All were smaller than he, lighter and narrower in the shoulder, each man with coal-black eyes, high cheekboned faces with hawklike features.

They were concentrating on a low hill and suddenly a rider came into view, a young woman with long, flowing hair the color of dry wheat. She rode an army horse and then, riding discreetly behind, at least twenty-five yards back, four troopers came into view. The girl rode well, her legs clad in riding britches, a dark-blue shirt covering breasts that swayed more than bounced. The tall, near-naked figure on the pinto watched as the six Mescalero moved their short-legged ponies, four fading back into the trees and hurrying in a half-circle while the other two slowly started toward the girl. He watched with his face growing tight, certain of what was going to happen and unable to prevent it. The two riders ahead of him stayed, let the girl draw closer, and then, with a sudden whoop and cry, they burst into the open and raced toward her.

He watched the four troopers instantly spur their horses forward as the girl slowed. They went into a full charge and swerved as one to intercept the two Mescalero. He knew that they thought the two Indians had failed to see them or were incredibly stupid. Their attention fully on the two Mescalero, they didn't even glance behind them as the four fast-racing Indian ponies swept out of the shadbush. When they suddenly realized they were being trapped, a volley of arrows had already cleaved the air and the first two Indians had wheeled their ponies to attack from the front. He saw two of the troopers go down with the first hail of arrows, then a third. The fourth soldier tried to race toward the girl, but the two Mescalero cut him off. He had his rifle up and fired, and one of the attackers fell from his pony.

The soldier tried to put himself between the attackers and the girl, but three arrows hurtled into him and he fell backward from his horse. He hit the ground, but, in a final display of discipline, managed to empty his gun and send the nearest attacker toppling from his pony. The girl tried to flee and lost valuable time trying to dodge and swerve. Two of the attackers came up alongside her, yanked her from the saddle, and she landed on the ground hard. She lay still for a moment, then rolled, shook the dry-wheat hair, and pushed to her feet. The four remaining Mescalero brought their ponies in a half-circle around her and began to herd her forward. She turned and walked on as they rode alongside and behind her, pushing her into the trees.

The girl walked proudly, defiantly, and the tall figure on the pinto remained motionless in the trees. He wouldn't leave her to that four. They were scavengers, rotten, thieving scavengers. His right hand touched the handle of the thin double-edged knife in the waistband of his breechclout. The four moved into the trees with the girl, and he slowly began to follow. He'd have to choose the right moment, he knew. He'd have but one chance. He stayed back. He had no need to see the four attackers and their captive. He could hear them as they moved through the woods, voices raised to exchange gruff grunts. They'd moved a few hundred yards when they suddenly stopped, and he heard a sharp cry of pain from the girl.

He slid from the pinto and hurried forward on silent, mountain cat's steps until they came into sight through the trees. They had dismounted and two held the girl while the other two faced her. One of them, taller than the others with mean, twisted lips, laughed as he slapped her across the face. Her head snapped around at the blow, the dry-wheat hair swirling, but she brought her eyes back to him and refused to show anything but defiance. He could see her properly for the first time: the shoulder-length hair framed a face of finely molded features, a thin, straight nose, fine, slightly thin lips, and eyebrows that arched upward over light-gray eyes.

He moved closer as the mean-mouthed one reached forward, stretched an arm out, and his hand closed around the neck of the dark-blue shirt. He pulled downward, the garment ripped apart, and cream-white breasts flashed into the open for an instant. But the girl twisted, tore away from her captors, and aimed a kick at the mean-mouthed one that caught him high on one leg. She tried to run, but a hand seized hold of the dry-wheat hair. She cried out in pain as she was flung to the ground. Two of the men pounced on her while the tallest one fell to his knees as he straddled her twisting body. He started to pull the riding britches open. All four now had their backs to the big man in the trees.

He took a long, silent step forward, the double-edged blade in his hand, and was almost upon the four men when one turned, suddenly sensing danger. The man's hand flew to the tomahawk at his waist, but the sharp, thin blade came down in a sideways arc, and his head almost fell from his neck. He collapsed as the line of red poured from his throat. The big man whirled and plunged the blade deep into the side of the tall, twisted-mouthed attacker as the man started to turn in surprise. The man's mouth came open as he staggered sideways and fell to the ground, his hand futilely trying to pull the blade from his side. But the other two had leaped up from the girl and came at him. One yanked a tomahawk from his waist, paused to take aim, and sent the short-handled ax hurtling through the air. The big man, with time to see the maneuver, waited a split second before dropping low, and the weapon sailed over his head. But he had to twist away from the charging second attacker, and he felt the man's hands brush his shoulders. He kicked out with one foot, caught the charging figure on one knee, and the man went down with a grunt of pain. The big man whirled and leapt forward. He brought his knee up hard, smashed it against the man's jaw, and the attacker's head snapped upward as he fell over in a backward arc.

The last attacker hurtled at him, a bone-scraping knife with jagged teeth held high. As the man came down with the knife, the near-naked, powerful form dove downward under the blow, slammed into the attacker's ankles, and the man did a somersault as his feet went out from under him and he catapulted forward. He hit the ground, the breath knocked out of him for a moment, tried to rise, and had time only to see the pile-driver blow smash down into his face. He gave a half cry, half grunt as it landed, shuddered for an instant, and lay still.

The big man whirled, saw the girl starting to run, and cut her off in a half dozen long-legged strides. She stopped, her light-gray eyes narrowing at him. "You're one of them. Why'd you stop them?" she asked. "You just want me all to yourself? Is that it?" He stared at the strong yet delicate loveliness of her. She had taken a moment to tie the torn pieces of the blue shirt together so that only the top, curving beauty of her creamy breasts showed. She stepped back as he said nothing, her eyes still narrowed, and he caught the tiny, despairing snort that fell from her lips. "What's the use. You don't understand a thing I've said," she murmured and took another step backward. He saw her eyes flick to a length of a stout branch that lay broken on the ground. She edged closer to it and he moved toward her. She halted, waited, and with a fury and quickness that failed to surprise him, she scooped the length of wood up in her hand and swung it at him.

He ducked, felt the club brush his hair, and lifted a short left uppercut that landed on the point of her lovely chin. She went down at once, eyes snapping closed. He stood over her and admired the smooth swell of one longish breast that all but fell from the torn and knotted shirt. He reached down, tore off another piece of her shirt tail, and made a gag for her mouth. She had a belt around her riding britches, and he took it off and tied her hands behind her back before he sat her against a tree trunk. He lowered himself to the ground across from her and waited until she came around, pulled her eyes open, and stared at him over the gag around her mouth. He rose, pulled her to her feet without anger, and led her to the pinto waiting in the woods. He sat her on the horse, swung on behind her, and felt the soft warmth of her rear against his groin. He rode slowly, unhurriedly, and she turned to look up at him, a frown of incomprehension on her face.

He went upward into the thick shadbush, swung north, and found a place that let him sweep the terrain below. It'd take time for the troopers he had toyed with to find their way back to the fort, and he guessed the day would be nearing an end before the chief of the soldiers sent his squads racing out to search for the girl. It would be a useless excursion, of course, and he almost smiled as he slid from the horse and lifted her to the ground. He sat down and pulled her to the ground beside him, his face impassive as he ignored the frowning stares she continued to turn at him. The sun had begun to slide in the afternoon sky when he saw the spirals of dust rise in the distance. Soon the soldiers came into view. Two full squads, he saw, one racing east, the other west. They would find the four troopers who had been slain, of course, but the remainder of their wild forays would bring them only sweat and anger.

He strained his eyes at the nearest squad, but he couldn't be certain if it was led by the chief of the soldiers himself. Finally the racing horses disappeared from view and the sun went below the horizon. He remained motionless until the moon came up high in the night sky. Finally he stood up, lifted the girl to her feet again, and put her on the pinto with him. He saw the questioning in her eyes as he slowly rode from the trees and down onto the flat, open land. He turned the pinto south, and another hour passed before he saw the shapes of the buildings of the town that edged out from one side of the fort. It was no great fort, he thought, its stockade walls only moderately high with no corner turrets. Yet it was reasonably strong, and he knew the sentries would be posted along the front walls. He sent the horse into a wide circle behind the fort, where he edged into a stand of rock and black oak.

He was directly at the rear of the fort when he halted, took the girl by the arm, and let her slide to the ground. He pointed at the fort and she gazed up at him. Why? her eyes questioned, and he saw gratefulness and relief mixed in with total incomprehension. He pointed to the fort again, and she began to walk, took a few steps backing up, and then turned and half ran toward the fort. He waited till she turned the rear corner on her way to the front gate before he moved the pinto backward in the trees and hurried silently away.

He allowed a smile to crease his face. She would have her answer soon enough.